Stories for Helen

Eliza Leslie

STORIES FOR HELEN

THE TELL-TALE.

ROSAMOND EVERING was one of those indiscreet mischievous girls who are in the daily practice of repeating every thing they see and hear; particularly all the unpleasant remarks, and unfavourable opinions that happen to be unguardedly expressed in their presence. She did not content herself with relating only as much as she actually saw and heard; but (as is always the case with tell-tales) she dealt greatly in exaggeration, and her stories never failed to exceed the reality in all their worst points.

This unamiable and dangerous propensity of their daughter, gave great pain to Mr. and Mrs. Evering, who tried in vain to correct it. They represented to her that as parents cannot be *constantly* on their guard in presence of their own family, and that as grown persons do not *always* remember or observe when children are in the room, many things are inadvertently said, which, though of little consequence as long as they remain unknown, may be of great and unfortunate importance if disclosed and exaggerated. And as children are incapable of forming an accurate judgment as to what may be told with safety, or what ought to be kept secret, their wisest and most proper course is to repeat no remarks and to relate no conversations whatever; but more particularly those which they may chance to hear from persons older than themselves.

But neither reproof nor punishment seemed to make any lasting impression on Rosamond Evering; and scarce a day passed that she did not exhibit some vexatious specimen of her besetting sin. A few instances will suffice.

Mrs. Evering had a very excellent cook, a black woman, that had lived with her more than six years, and whom she considered an invaluable servant. One morning, when Venus (for that was her name) had just left the parlour, after receiving her orders for dinner, Mr. Evering remarked, in a low voice, to his lady, "Certainly, the name of Venus was never so unsuitably bestowed as on this poor woman. I have rarely seen a negro whose face had a greater resemblance to that of a baboon." In this remark Mrs. Evering acquiesced.

Rosamond was at this time sitting in a corner, looking over her lessons. Just before she went to school, her mother thought of a change in the preparations for dinner, and not wishing to give the old cook the trouble of coming up from the kitchen a second time, she desired Rosamond to go down and tell Venus she would have the turkey boiled rather than roasted. Rosamond went down and delivered the message; but fixing her eyes on the cook's face, she thought she had never seen Venus look so ugly, and she said to her, "Venus, my father thinks you are the ugliest negro he ever saw (*even for a negro*) and he says your face is just like a monkey's, only worse." Having made this agreeable communication, Rosamond went out of the kitchen and departed for school, leaving Venus speechless with anger and astonishment; for though in other respects a very good woman, she was extremely vain, and had always considered herself among the handsomest of her race.

As soon as Venus found herself able to speak, she went into the parlour with her eyes flashing fire, and told Mrs. Evering that she must provide herself with another cook, as she was determined to leave her that very day. Mrs. Evering with much surprise inquired the reason, and Venus replied, that "she would not live in any house where she was called an ugly neger, the ugliest even of all negers, and likened to a brute beast."

Mrs. Evering, who had forgotten her husband's remark, asked the cook what she meant; and Venus explained by repeating all that Rosamond had told her. Mrs. Evering endeavoured to pacify her, but in vain. Ignorant people when once offended are very difficult to appease, and Venus had been hurt on the tenderest point. She would listen to nothing that Mrs. Evering could urge to induce her to stay; but exclaimed in a high passion, "I never was called a neger before. I am not a neger but a coloured woman. I was born and raised on a great plantation in Virginny where there was hundreds of slaves, all among the Randolphs and sich like quality, and nobody never called me a neger. And now when I'm free, and come here to Philadelphy where nobody has no servants without they hires them, lo! and behold, I'm called a neger, and an ugly neger too, and a neger-monkey besides. No, no, I'll not stay; and Nancy the chambermaid may do the cooking till you get somebody else. And a pretty way she'll do it in. I'm glad I shan't be here to eat Nancy's cooking. I never know'd any *white trash* that could cook; much less Irish."

Finally, Mrs. Evering was obliged to give Venus her wages and let here go at once, as she protested "she would never eat another meal's victuals in the house."

When Rosamond came from school, her mother reprimanded her severely; and when her father heard of the mischief she had caused, he would not permit her to accompany the family to a concert that evening, as she had been promised the day before.

After the departure of Venus, it was a long time before Mrs. Evering could suit herself with a cook. Several were tried in succession but none were good; and to Rosamond's great regret, they were never able to get a woman whose skill in making pies, and puddings, and cakes, bore any comparison to that of Venus.

Still this lesson did not cure her fault; she still told tales, and still suffered in consequence.

One day, Mrs. Renwick, a lady who lived next door, sent a message to Mrs. Evering, requesting that she would lend her a pot of red currant jelly, as she was quite out of that article, of which she shortly intended making a supply; and as Mr. Renwick had invited some company to dinner, some jelly would be wanted to eat with the canvass-back ducks.

Mrs. Evering lent her a pot, and as soon as currants were in the market, Mrs. Renwick sent her in return some jelly of her own making. It was not nice, and Mrs. Evering observed to her sister, Mrs. Norwood, who happened to be present: "I do not think Mrs. Renwick has been very successful with her jelly. It is so thin it is almost liquid, and so dark that it looks as if made of black currants. I suspect she has boiled it too long, and has not put in sugar enough."

Next day as they were coming from school together, Mrs. Renwick's little daughter, Marianne, said to Rosamond, "My mother made some currant jelly on Tuesday, and yesterday when it was cold, she gave me a whole saucer-full to eat with my slice of bread, at twelve o'clock."

"She might well give you a whole saucer-full," replied Rosamond, "for I do not think it was worth saving for any better purpose. She sent in a pot to my mother, in return for some she had borrowed of her. Now *my* mother's jelly is always so firm that you might cut it with a knife, and so bright and sparkling that it dazzles your eyes. I heard her tell my aunt Norwood, that Mrs. Renwick's jelly was the worst she had ever seen, that it was as thin and sour as plain currant juice, and dark and dirty-looking beside."

Marianne Renwick was much displeased at the disrespectful manner in which her mother's jelly had been spoken of. She let go Rosamond's arm, and turning up another street, walked home by herself, swelling with resentment, and told her mother all that had passed.

Mrs. Renwick was a lady very easily offended; and she always signified her anger as soon as she felt it. She immediately sent to a confectioner's for a pot of the very best red currant jelly, and had it carried into Mrs. Evering; accompanied by a note implying "that she regretted to hear that her jelly had not been so fortunate as to meet the approbation of so competent a judge of sweetmeats; but that, as she would be sorry if Mrs. Evering should lose any thing by it, she had sent her a pot made by one of the very first confectioners in the city; and she hoped it would be found an ampleequivalent for that she had most unhappily borrowed."

Rosamond was in the parlour when the note and the pot of jelly arrived, and she coloured and looked so confused, that her mother immediately guessed she had been the cause of Mrs. Renwick's having taken offence. Reproof had no effect on Rosamond except for a moment; but that she might frequently be reminded of her fault, she was not allowed to taste currant jelly till the next summer. Mrs. Renwick, however, remained implacable; and could never be prevailed on to visit Mrs. Evering again.

Mr. Evering had an aunt, the widow of a western merchant who had made a large fortune in business. After the death of her husband, Mrs. Marbury had removed to Philadelphia, which was her native place; and, being very plain in her habits and ideas, she had bought a small neat house in a retired street, where she kept but two servants, and expended more money in presents to her relations, than in any superfluities for herself. She generally went to a place of worship in her own neighbourhood; but hearing that a very celebrated minister from Boston was to preach one Sunday in the church to which her nephew's family belonged, she sent a message to Mr. Evering requesting that he would call for her with his carriage and give her a seat in his pew, that she might have an opportunity of hearing this distinguished stranger. Mr. and Mrs. Evering were both out when the message arrived, so that no answer could be sent till their return; which was not till evening.

It was dusk, and the lamps not being yet lighted, they did not perceive that Rosamond was lying on an ottoman in one of the recesses, or they would not have spoken as they did while she was present.

"I am very sorry," said Mrs. Evering, "that Mrs. Marbury has fixed on to-morrow for going to church with us, for I intended asking Miss Leeson, who will be delighted to have an opportunity of hearing this celebrated preacher; and his discourse, however excellent, will be lost on aunt Marbury, who always falls asleep soon after she has heard the text, that being all she ever remembers of a sermon. So that in reality, one preacher is the same to her as another; though she goes regularly to church twice a-day, and never could be convinced that she sleeps half the time. And then she is unfortunately so fat, and takes up so much room in the pew."

"My dear," said Mr. Evering, "we must show Mrs. Marbury as much kindness and civility as we possibly can, for she is a most excellent woman, is very liberal to us now, and at her death will undoubtedly leave us the greatest part of her large property. Even if we had no personal regard for the good old lady, it would be very impolitic in us to offend her."

When the room was lighted, Mr. and Mrs. Evering saw Rosamond on the ottoman, and felt so much uneasiness at her having heard their conversation, that they thought it best to caution her against repeating it. "Oh!" exclaimed Rosamond, "do you think I would be so wicked as to tell aunt Marbury what you have just been saying about her?"

"You have often," said Mrs. Evering, "told things almost as improper to be repeated."

"But never with any bad intention," replied Rosamond, "I am sure my feelings are always good."

"I know not," said her father, "how it is possible that people with good feelings and good intentions can take pleasure in repeating whatever they hear to a person's disadvantage, and above all to the very object of the unfavourable remarks. Beside the cruelty of causing them poignant and unnecessary pain, and wounding their self-love, there is the wickedness of embroiling them with their friends; or at least destroying their confidence, and imbittering their hearts. And all these consequences have frequently ensued from the tattling of a tell-tale child."

The next morning was Saturday; and the servants being all very busy, Mrs. Evering desired Rosamond to stop, as she returned from taking her music-lesson, and inform her aunt Marbury that they would be happy to accommodate her with a seat in their pew on Sunday morning; and that they would call for her in the carriage, as she had requested.

"Now, Rosamond," said Mrs. Evering, "can I trust you? Will you, for once, be discreet, and refrain from repeating to your aunt Marbury, what you unluckily overheard last evening?"

"O! indeed, dear mother," replied Rosamond, "bad as you think me, I am not quite wicked enough for that."

"But I fear the force of habit," said Mrs. Evering. "I believe I had better send Peter with the message."

"No," answered Rosamond, "I am anxious to retrieve my character. Rely on me this once; and you will see how prudent and honourable I can be."

On her way home from her music-lesson, Rosamond stopped at her aunt's, and delivered the message, exactly as it had been given to her.

While Rosamond was eating a piece of the nice plum-cake that her aunt always kept in the house for the gratification of her young visitors, Mrs. Marbury said to her, "This weather is quite too warm for the season; should it continue, it will be very oppressive in church to-morrow."

"No doubt," answered Rosamond, "and most probably *our* church will be crowded in every part. I wonder, aunt, that you are anxious to go, as you certainly *must* be, when you sent so long beforehand to engage a seat in our pew."

"In truth," returned Mrs. Marbury, "I am willing to suffer some inconvenience from the heat, for the sake of hearing this great preacher."

"But, aunt," said Rosamond, "if you get sleepy, you will not hear him after all."

"O!" replied Mrs. Marbury, "I am never sleepy in church. I am always so attentive that I never feel in the least drowsy."

"O! indeed, aunt, I have often seen you asleep in church," exclaimed Rosamond.

"Impossible, Rosamond, impossible," cried Mrs. Marbury. "You are entirely mistaken. It must have been merely your own imagination."

"Why, dear aunt," said Rosamond, "my father and mother, as well as myself, have all seen you asleep in church. If it was not true, the whole family could not imagine it. It was but last evening, I heard my mother say, that she wished you had not taken a notion to go to church with us on Sunday, as it would prevent her from inviting Miss Leeson, whom she likes far better than you. She said, beside, that fat people take up so much room, that they are always encumbrances every where; and that there was no use at all in your going to church, as you slept soundly all the time you were there, and even breathed so hard as to disturb the congregation."

"And what did your father say to all this?" asked Mrs. Marbury, turning very pale, and looking much shocked and mortified.

"My father," answered Rosamond, "said that, on account of your money, we must endure you, and all the inconveniences belonging to you; for if you were kept in good humour, he had no doubt of your leaving him all your property when you die."

Mrs. Marbury looked aghast. She burst into tears, and Rosamond, finding that she had gone quite too far, vainly attempted to pacify her.

"You may go home, child," exclaimed Mrs. Marbury, sobbing with anger, "you may go home, and tell your father and mother that I shall not trouble them with my company at church or any where else; and when I die, I shall leave my money to the hospital or to some other institution. How have I been deceived! But I shall take care in future not to bestow my affection on those that have any expectations from me."

Rosamond, now very much frightened, declared that she could not take such a message to her parents; and begged her aunt to screen her from their displeasure, by not informing them of the communication she had so indiscreetly made.

Her alarm and agitation were so great, that Mrs. Marbury consented, out of pity, not to betray her to her father and mother; and to excuse herself from going to church with them (which she declared she could never do again) by alleging the heat of the weather, and the probable crowd.

"And now, Rosamond," said her aunt Marbury, "do not think that I feel at all obliged to you for having opened my eyes as to the manner in which your parents really regard me. Their behaviour to me, as far as I could judge for myself, has always been exactly what I wished it; and if their kindness was not sincere, I still thought it so, and was happy in being deceived. And now, after what you have told me, how can I again think of them as I have hitherto done? You have acted basely towards them in repeating their private conversation, and cruelly to your kind aunt, in giving her unnecessary pain and mortification. You have caused much mischief; and who has been the gainer? Not yourself certainly. You have lost my good opinion, for I can never like a tell-tale. I had heard something of your being addicted to this vice; but till now I could not believe it. I shall not betray you to your parents, though you have so shamefully betrayed *them* to *me*. But you may rely on it, that sooner or later the discovery will be made, to your utter shame and confusion. Now you may go home, with the assurance that you can no longer be a welcome visitor at my house."

Rosamond departed, overwhelmed with compunction; and in the resolution (which she had so often made and so often broken) never again to be guilty of a similar fault. She gave her aunt's message to her parents, and Miss Leeson was invited to accompany them next day to church.

Two days after, Mrs. Evering went to visit Mrs. Marbury, and to her great surprise heard from the servants that she had left town with some western friends who were returning home; and that she purposed being absent from Philadelphia five or six months; dividing her time among various places on the other side of the Alleghanies, and probably extending her tour to Louisiana, where she owned some land.

Her going away so suddenly without apprising them of her intention, was totally inexplicable to Mr. and Mrs. Evering; and they justly concluded that she must have taken some offence. Rosamond well knew the cause, and rightly supposed that her aunt finding herself unable to meet the family with her former feelings towards them, had thought it best to avoid seeing them for a very long time.

The confusion visible in Rosamond's face and manner when Mrs. Marbury was spoken of, aroused the suspicions of her father and mother: and on their questioning her closely, she confessed, with many tears, that she had really informed her aunt of what had passed on the subject of her accompanying them to church. But as tell-tales have very little candour where themselves are concerned, and as tale-telling always leads to lying, she steadily denied that she had been guilty of the slightest exaggeration in her report to Mrs. Marbury; protesting that she had told her nothing but the simple truth.

From that time, Rosamond was not allowed to visit or call at any house unaccompanied by her mother, who was almost afraid to trust her out of her sight. Her parents avoided discussing any thing of the least consequence in *her* presence; always remembering to send her out of the room. This mode of treatment very much mortified her; but she could not help acknowledging that she deserved it.

Her father received no intelligence from Mrs. Marbury. He and Mrs. Evering both wrote to her at different times, endeavouring to mollify her displeasure; but not knowing exactly where she was, the letters were not directed to the right places, and did not reach her.

For a long time Rosamond was so unusually discreet, that her parents began to hope that her odious fault was entirely cured.

One day, her chamber having been washed in the afternoon, it was found too damp for her to sleep in with safety to her health; and her mother told her that she must, that night, occupy the room adjoining hers. This room, which was but seldom used, was separated from Mrs. Evering's apartment by a very thin partition; and communicated with it by a door which was almost always kept closed; the bed in each of these chambers being placed against it.

Rosamond, having been awakened in the night by the fighting of some cats in the yard, heard her father and mother in earnest conversation. They had totally forgotten her vicinity to them; and as tell-tales are never wanting in curiosity, she sat up in her bed and applying her ear to the key-hole of the door, she distinctly heard every word they said, though they were speaking in a low voice.

She was soon able to comprehend the subject of their conversation. Mr. Evering was lamenting that the failure of a friend for whom he had endorsed to a large amount, had brought him into unexpected difficulties; but he hoped that he would be able to go on till the sums due to him by some western merchants should arrive.

Next evening, Rosamond was permitted to go to a juvenile cotillon-party, held once a fortnight, at the ball-room of her dancing-master. To this place her mother always accompanied her; and while Mrs. Evering was sitting in conversation with some ladies, a boy named George Granby, who was frequently the partner of Rosamond at these balls, came up and asked her to dance. They were obliged to go to the farthest end of the room before they could get places in a cotillon; and while they were waiting for the music to begin, George, who thought Rosamond a very pretty girl, asked her if she would also be his partner in the country-dance. She replied that Henry Harford had engaged her, at the last ball, for this country-dance.

"Oh!" replied George Granby, "Henry Harford will not be here to-night; his father failed yesterday."

"True," said Rosamond, "I wonder I should have forgotten Mr. Harford's failure, when my father lost so much by him. But when the fathers fail, must the children stay away from balls?"

"Certainly," replied George, "it would be considered very improper for the family to be seen in any place of amusement when its head is in so much trouble, and when they have lost all they possessed."

"O then," exclaimed Rosamond, "I hope *my* father will not fail till the cotillon-parties are over for the season. There are but two more, and I should be very sorry to give them up. I hope he will be able to go on, at least till after that time. How sorry I shall be when he *does* fail."

"I believe you," said George; "but what makes you talk about your father's failing? I thought he was considered safe enough."

"Ah! you know but little about it," answered Rosamond. "I heard him tell my mother last night, that he was in hourly dread of failing, in consequence of the great losses by Mr. Harford, and of his own business having gone on badly for a long time. However, say nothing about it, for such things ought not to be told."

"They ought not, indeed," said the boy.

As soon as George Granby went home, he repeated what he had heard from Rosamond, to his father, who was one of Mr. Evering's creditors. The consequence was, that Mr. Granby and all the principal creditors took immediate measures to secure themselves; and Mr. Evering (who could have gone on till he got through his difficulties, had he been allowed time, and had the state of his affairs remained unsuspected,) became a bankrupt through the worse than indiscretion of his daughter. Had Mrs. Marbury been in town, or where he could have had speedy communication with her, he doubted not that she would have lent him assistance to ward off the impending blow. But she had gone away in a fit of displeasure, occasioned, also, by the tattling of Rosamond.

Mr. Granby, who was the chief creditor and a man of contracted feelings and great severity, showed no liberality on the occasion; and proceeded to the utmost extremity that the law would warrant. Every article of Mr. Evering's property was taken; and indeed, since it had come to this, his principles would not allow him to reserve any thing whatever from his creditors.

The scene that ensued in the Evering family, on the day following the ball, can better be imagined than described. Mr. Granby had at once informed Mr. Evering of the source from whence he had derived his information with respect to the posture of his affairs; and when Rosamond found this new and terrible proof of the fatal effects of her predominant vice, she went into an hysteric fit, and was so ill all night, that her parents, in addition to their other troubles, had to fear for the life of their daughter. The sufferings of her mind brought on a fever; and it was more than a week before she was able to leave her bed.

Her father and mother kindly forgave her, and avoided all reference to her fault. But she could not forgive herself, and on the day that they left their handsome residence in one of the principal streets, and removed to a small mean-looking house in the suburbs, her agony was more than words can express. All their furniture was sold at auction, even Rosamond's piano, and her mother's work-table. Their most expensive articles of clothing were put away, as in their present circumstances it would be improper to wear them. The house they now inhabited, contained only one little parlour with a kitchen back of it, and three small rooms upstairs. Their furniture was limited to what was barely useful, and of the cheapest kind. Their table was as plain as possible; and their only servant a very young half-grown girl.

This sad change in their way of living, added to the stings of self-reproach, almost broke Rosamond's heart; and her pride was much shocked when she found that her father had applied for the situation of clerk in a counting-house, as a means of supporting his family till something better should offer.

At length Mrs. Marbury returned; having hurried back to Philadelphia as soon as the intelligence of her nephew's failure had reached her. How did she blame herself for having taken such serious offence at what now appeared to her almost too trifling to remember. All her former regard for the Evering family returned. She sought them immediately in their humble retreat, and offered Mr. Evering her assistance to the utmost farthing she could command.

To conclude, Mr. Evering's affairs were again put in train. He resumed his business; and a few years restored him to his former situation.

This sad, but salutary lesson produced a lasting effect on Rosamond; and from that time, she kept so strict a watch over her ruling passion, that she succeeded in entirely eradicating it. She grew up a discreet and amiable girl; and no one who knew her in after years, could have believed that till the age of fourteen she had been an incorrigible tell-tale.

THE BOARDING-SCHOOL FEAST.

"They hear a voice in every wind,And snatch a fearful joy."

IT is a very common subject of complaint with boarding-school children (and there is often sufficient foundation for it) that they are too much restricted in their food, and that their diet is not only inferior in quality to what it ought to be, but frequently deficient in quantity also. There was certainly, however, no cause for any dissatisfaction of this sort at Mrs. Middleton's boarding-school, in Philadelphia. The table was in every respect excellent; and a basket of bread or biscuit, and sometimes of gingerbread, was handed round to all the pupils, every morning at eleven o'clock. Mrs. Middleton's young ladies were strangers to the common boarding-school practice of coaxing or bribing the servants to procure them cakes and tarts from the confectioners; for the table was sufficiently supplied with those articles, made in such a manner as to be agreeable to the taste without endangering the health; and they were every day allowed some sort of fruit, of the best quality the market could furnish.

At last, a young lady named Henrietta Harwood became a member of Mrs. Middleton's seminary. Miss Harwood had been for several years a pupil of one of those too numerous establishments, where the comfort of the children is sacrificed to the vanity of a governess, who rests her claims to encouragement principally on the merits of elegantly furnished parlours, an expensive style of dress, frequent evening parties, and occasional balls. In schools where outward show is the leading principle, the internal economy is generally conducted on the most parsimonious plan, and while the masters (who attend only at certain hours) are such as are considered the most fashionable, the female teachers that live in the house, are too often vulgar girls obtained at a low salary, and who frequently are in league with the elder pupils in ridiculing and plotting against the governess.

Most of the faults and follies that were likely to be acquired at a show-boarding-school, Henrietta Harwood brought with her to the excellent and well-conducted establishment of Mrs. Middleton: but she had some redeeming qualities that made her rather a favourite with her new companions, and disposed her governess to hope that all would come right at last.

One evening, the elder young ladies were sitting very comfortably at their different occupations, round the table in the front school-room. The window-shutters were closed, a good fire was burning in the stove, and Mrs. Middleton had just sent them a basket of apples, according to her custom in the winter evenings. After finishing a very fine one, Henrietta Harwood exclaimed—"Well—I wonder at myself for eating these apples!"

Miss Brownlow. Why, I am sure they are the very best Newtown pippins.

Henrietta. That is true, Brownie: but at Madame Disette's we had something better of evenings than mere apples.

Miss Brownlow. What had you?

Henrietta. We had sometimes cheesecakes, and sometimes tarts; with very frequently pound-cake and jumbles; and sometimes we had even little mince-pies, and oyster-patties.

Miss Wilcox. O, delicious! What an excellent governess! How could you ever consent to leave her? I thought Mrs. Middleton allowed us a great many good things; but she does not send us cheesecakes and tarts of an evening.

Henrietta. O, do not mistake! We might have gone without them all our lives, before Madame Disette would have sent us any thing of the sort. She did not even allow us apples of an evening, or a piece of bread between breakfast and dinner. Why, one summer evening, she bought at the door some common ice-cream, of a black man that was carrying it through the streets in a tin pot; and when we thought that, *for once,* she had certainly treated us, she charged the ice-cream in our quarter-bills. No, no,—we got nothing from *her,* but stale bread; bad butter; sloppy tea; coffee without taste or colour; skinny meat, half-cooked one day, cold the next, and hashed or rather coddled the third. Then, for a dessert, we were regaled with sour knotty apples in the winter, worm-eaten cherries in the summer, and dry squashy pears in the autumn; and once a week we had boiled rice, or baked bread and milk, by way of pudding. Though after the scholars had eaten their allowance, and made their curtsies and gone up to the school-room, she always had something nice brought for herself, and her sister, and niece: and of which poor Benson, the under teacher, was never invited to partake.

Miss Wilcox. But how did you get such nice things in the evening?

Henrietta. We bought them, to be sure: bought them with our own money. That was the only way. When the little girls had all gone to bed, and Madame Disette, and Madame Trompeur, and Mademoiselle Mensonge were engaged in the parlour with their company, we all (that is, the first class) subscribed something; and we commissioned the chambermaid to bring us whatever we wanted from the confectioner's. O, what delightful feasts we had!

Miss Thomson. Did Madame Disette never find you out?

Henrietta. O, no!—we laid our plans too cunningly. And Benson, the teacher, was a good creature, and always joined our party; so we knew she would not tell.

Miss Scott. I am sure we never could prevail on our teacher, Miss Loxley, to be concerned in such things. *She* would think it so very improper.

Henrietta. Well, we must take an opportunity when Miss Loxley is not at home. Mrs. Middleton permits her to go out whenever she requests it. She does not keep her so closely confined as Madame Disette did poor Benson.

Miss Scott. Mrs. Middleton has so much reliance on her elder pupils, that she is not afraid to trust us sometimes without Miss Loxley. And we, certainly, have never yet abused her confidence.

Henrietta. O, you are undoubtedly a most exemplary set! But you never had one like *me* among you. I shall soon put a little spirit into you all, and get you out of this strict-propriety sort of way. I do not despair even of my friend Isabella Caldwell, the good girl of the school.

Isabella. Our way is a very satisfactory one. It is impossible for boarding-school girls to be happier than we are. Our minds are not exhausted with long and difficult lessons, and with studies beyond our capacity. When school-hours are over, we have full time for recreation, and are amply provided with the means of amusing ourselves. We have a library of entertaining books; and we have liberty to divert ourselves with all sorts of juvenile plays and games. Then how much attention is paid to our health and our comforts, and how kindly and judiciously are we treated in every respect! Certainly, we ought to think ourselves happy.

Henrietta. Ay! so you are made to say in the letters which you write home to your parents. All our French letters, at Madame Disette's were written first by her niece Mademoiselle Mensonge; and the English letters were manufactured by poor Benson; and then we copied them in our very best hands, with a new pen at every paragraph. They were all nearly the same; and told of nothing but the superabundant kindness and liberality of Madame Disette, our high respect and esteem for Madame Trompeur, her sister, and our vast affection for her amiable niece, Mademoiselle Mensonge: together with our perfect health, and extreme felicity. In every letter we grew happier and happier.

Miss Snodgrass. And were you not so in reality?

Henrietta. No, indeed,—all the happiness we had was of our own making, for we derived none from any thing our governess did for us; though we were obliged in our letters to call her our beloved Madame Disette, and to express the most fervent hopes that we might one day exactly resemble her; which, I am sure, was the last thing we could have desired; for she was one of the ugliest women that I ever saw in my life.

Miss Thomson. But you might have wished to resemble her in mind and manners.

Henrietta. Why, as to that, her mind was worse than her face, and her manners we all thought absolutely ridiculous. Benson could mimic her exactly.

Miss Marley. I do not wonder that your parents took you away from such a school.

Henrietta. The school was certainly bad enough. We had dirty, uncomfortable chambers; scanty fires; a mean table, and all such inconveniences. But then it was a very fashionable school; all the masters were foreigners, and above all things there was a great point made of our speaking French. We knew the common phrases perfectly well. We could all say, *Comment vous portez vous,—Je vous remerçie,—Il fait beau-temps,—Donnez-moi un epingle,—Lequel aimez-vous mieux, le bleu ou le vert?* and many other things equally sensible and interesting. This was what was called French conversation, and we were all able to join in it, after taking lessons in French a very few quarters.

But after all, we had a great deal of fun, and that made up for every thing. Madame Disette and her sister and niece, always hurried over the school-business as fast as possible, that they might have time to pay and receive visits; and every evening they were either out, or engaged at home with company; so that we had nobody to watch us but poor Benson, and none of us cared for *her.* And then we could make her do just as we pleased. She only got seventy-five dollars a year, for which she was obliged to perform all the drudgery of the school, even to washing and dressing the little girls; putting them to bed; darning their stockings and mending their clothes; besides doing all Madame Disette's plain sewing. Poor Benson could not afford to dress half so well as the chambermaid. So how could we have any respect for her? Even the servants despised her, and never would do any thing she asked them.

Miss Snodgrass. Well, we all respect Miss Loxley. She gets a good salary, dresses genteelly, is treated with proper consideration by every one in the house, and we obey her just as we do Mrs. Middleton.

Henrietta. Yes, and for those very reasons, we never can ask her to assist in any little private scheme of our own. Benson was certainly a much more convenient person. But to resume our first subject—I do really long for a feast.

Miss Roberts. Well,—Mrs. Middleton occasionally gives us a feast as you call it; for instance, on the birth-day of the young lady who is head of her class.

Henrietta. O, but then at these regular feasts Mrs. Middleton is always present herself. I like to steal a little secret pleasure, unsuspected by any one that would check it. Ah! you have never dealt in mysteries; you know not how delightful they are. One half the enjoyment is in planning and carrying on the plot. Come now, girls, let us get up a little feast to-morrow evening. You know Miss Loxley will be out again, as her aunt is still sick; and the French teacher always goes home at dusk, as she does not sleep here.

Miss Watkins. But if Mrs. Middleton should discover us.

Henrietta. No. Her sister and brother-in-law are coming to spend the evening with her, and to bring a lady and gentleman from Connecticut. To-morrow is the very best night we can possibly have. Leave it all to me, and I will engage that there shall be no discovery; and we will get the little girls to bed very early, that we may have the longer time to enjoy ourselves.

Several of the young ladies. O, indeed we are afraid!

Henrietta. Nonsense—I will answer for it that there shall be no cause for fear. Why, we did these things fifty times at Madame Disette's, and were never once detected. Come, I will lay down a dollar as the first contribution towards the feast. Brownie, how much will you give?

Miss Brownlow. I will give half a dollar.

Miss Watkins. And I will give a dollar and a half. I have always plenty of money.

Henrietta. Well done, Watty. And you Scotty, how much?

Miss Scott. A quarter of a dollar is all I have left.

Miss Wilcox. And I have only ten cents.

Henrietta. O, poor Coxey! But never mind, you shall have as large a share of the good things as any of us, notwithstanding you can only muster ten cents. And now, Snoddy?

Miss Snodgrass. Why, I will give a quarter of a dollar and eight cents. I have another quarter of a dollar, but I wish to keep it to buy a bottle of Cologne water.

Henrietta. Pho.—Try to live another week without the Cologne.

Miss Snodgrass. No indeed,—I never in my life had a bottle of Cologne water all to myself, to use just as I pleased; and I really have set my mind on it.

Henrietta. Well, we must try to do without Snoddy's other quarter-dollar. Well, Bob, what say you?

Miss Roberts. I will give half a dollar.

Henrietta. O, Bob, Bob! You have more than that, I am sure.

Miss Roberts. Yes, I have another half dollar, but I wish to buy the book of Fairy Tales you told me of.

Henrietta. O, never mind buying the Fairy Tales! I will tell you all of them without charging for my trouble. Come now, be good and give the whole dollar, and we will have an iced pound-cake.

Miss Roberts. Well, if you will *certainly* tell me all the Fairy Tales.

Henrietta. Every one of them; twice over if you choose. And now, Marley.

Miss Marley. I know all this is very improper.

Henrietta. Just for once in your life try how it seems to be improper.

Miss Marley. Well then for this time only—Here are three quarters of a dollar.

Henrietta. Now, Tommy!

Miss Thomson. I have not resolution to resist. There are half a dollar and twelve cents.

Henrietta. And now, Isabella Caldwell,—though last not least.

Isabella. Excuse me, Henrietta: my contribution will be far less than that of any other young lady. In fact, nothing at all.

Henrietta. Nothing at all! Why Miss Caldwell, I did not expect this of you! I always supposed you to be very generous.

Isabella. I wish to be generous whenever it is in my power.

Henrietta. Well, dear Isabella, if you have no money, we will not press you. We shall be happy to have you at our little feast, even if you do not contribute a cent towards it.

All. O, yes! We must not lose Isabella Caldwell.

Isabella. I am much obliged to you, my dear girls. But it is not the want of money that prevents me from joining you. I *have* money. But I wish not, on any terms, to belong to your party; and I shall retire to my own room. In short, I do not think it right to be planning a feast without the knowledge of Mrs. Middleton, who is so good and so indulgent that it is a shame to deceive her.

Henrietta. Then I suppose. Miss Caldwell, you intend to betray us; to disclose the whole plan to Mrs. Middleton?

Isabella. You insult me by such a suspicion. I appeal to all the young ladies if they ever knew me guilty of telling tales, or repeating any thing which might be a disadvantage to another.

All. O, no, no! Isabella is to be trusted. She will never betray us.

Henrietta. Then in plain terms, Miss Caldwell, I really think, if you have money, you might spare a little for our feast.

Isabella. I want the whole of it for another purpose. And I shall get no more before next week.

Henrietta. Well, this is very strange. I know you do not care for finery, and that you never lay out your pocket-money in little articles of dress. And as for books of amusement, it was but yesterday that your father sent you a whole box full. I *must* say, that though you are called generous—I cannot help thinking you a little—a very little—

Isabella. Mean, I suppose you would say.

Henrietta. Why, I must not exactly call you *mean*—But I cannot help thinking you rather—*meanish.*

Isabella. I will not be called mean. My refusal proceeds from other motives than you suppose.

Henrietta. Young ladies, I will be judged by you all. Is it natural for a girl of fifteen, who likes cakes, and pastry, and every sort of sweet thing, to be so very conscientious as to refuse to join in a little bit of pleasure that can injure no one, that will never be discovered, and that all her companions have assented to with few or no scruples. No, no, Isabella, I believe that your only object in declining to be one of our party, is to save your money.

Isabella. O, what injustice you do me!

Henrietta. Prove it to be injustice by joining us without further objection.

Miss Watkins. Henrietta, we do not care for Isabella's money. Let her keep it if she wishes. We can afford to entertain her as our guest. I am sorry so much should have been said about it.

Isabella (*taking her purse out of her bag.*) There then; here are two half-dollars. I will prove to you that I am neither mean nor selfish.

All. We will not take your money.

Isabella. Yes, take it.—Any thing rather than suspect me of what I do not deserve. And now let me entreat, that in *my* presence nothing more may be said of this feast. Change the subject, and talk of something else. Or, rather, I will retire to bed, and leave you to make your arrangements for to-morrow night.

The real reason why Isabella Caldwell was so unwilling to be a contributor to the expense of the feast, was, that she had intended appropriating her pocket-money to a much better purpose. Her allowance was a dollar a week; and she knew that a coloured woman, named Diana, (who had formerly been a servant in her father's family before they removed to the country) was now struggling with severe poverty. Diana was the widow of a negro sailor who had perished at sea, and she was the mother of three children, all too small to put out, and whom she supported by taking in washing. But during a long illness brought on by overworking herself, she lost several of her customers who had given their washing to others. Isabella had solicited Mrs. Middleton to allow her to employ Diana, rather than the woman who then washed for the school. Mrs. Middleton readily consented.

The weather had become very cold, and Isabella saw with regret that Diana came to fetch and carry the clothes-bag without either coat or cloak; nothing in fact to cover her shoulders but an old yellow cotton shawl. Isabella pitied her extremely, and resolved in her own mind not to lay out a cent of her money till she had saved enough to buy Diana a cloak. Her father, who was a man of large fortune, had placed, at the beginning of the year, a sum of money in Mrs. Middleton's hands to defray Isabella's expenses, exclusive of her tuition; with directions to give her every week a dollar to dispose of as she pleased.

Isabella had now been saving her money for four weeks, and had that morning received her weekly allowance, which completed the sum necessary to buy a good plaid cloak, and she had determined to go the following morning and make the purchase, and to give it to Diana when she came to take the clothes. Isabella had now the exact money; and that was the reason she was so unwilling to devote any part of it to the expenses of the feast. Beside which, she could not, in her heart, approve of any species of pleasure that was to be enjoyed in secret, and kept from the knowledge of her excellent governess. She felt the usual repugnance of modest and benevolent people with regard to speaking of her own acts of charity. This reluctance she, however, carried too far, when rather than acknowledge that she was keeping her money to buy a cloak for her poor washerwoman, she suffered herself to be prevailed on to give up part of the sum, as an addition to the fund that was raising for the banquet.

She went to bed sadly out of spirits, and much displeased with herself. She had seen at a store, just such a cloak as she wished to get for Diana; and she had anticipated the delight and gratitude of the poor woman on receiving it, and the comfort it would afford her during the inclement season, and for many succeeding winters. "And now," thought she, "poor Diana must go without a cloak, and the money will be wasted in cakes and tarts; which, however nice they may be, will cause us no further pleasure after we have once swallowed them. However, perhaps the weather will be less severe to-morrow; and next week I shall have another dollar, and I then will again be able to buy Diana the cloak. I am sorry that I promised it to her when she was here last. I cannot bear the idea of seeing her, and telling her that she must wait for the cloak a week longer. I hope the weather will be mild and fine to-morrow."

But Isabella's hope was not realized; and when she rose in the morning, she found it snowing very fast. The cold was intense. The ground had been for several days already covered with a deep snow which had frozen very hard. There was a piercing north-east wind; and, altogether, it was the most inclement morning of the whole winter. Isabella hoped that Diana would not come for the clothes that day, as the weather would be a sufficient excuse; though the poor woman had never before been otherwise than punctual. But in a short time, she saw Diana coming round the corner, walking very fast, her arms wrapped in her shawl, and holding down her head to avoid, as much as possible, the snow that was driving in her face. "Ah!" thought Isabella, "she hopes to get the cloak this dreadful morning, and to wear it home. How sadly she will be disappointed! But I cannot see or speak to her." She then tied up her clothes-bag, and desired the chambermaid to take it down and give it to Diana, and tell her that she could not see her that morning.

Isabella could not forbear going again to the window; and she saw Diana come up the area steps into the street, carrying the clothes-bag, and looking disappointed. Isabella, with a heavy heart, watched her till she turned the corner, shrinking from the storm, and shivering along in her old thin shawl. "Oh!" thought Isabella, "how very badly the confectionary will taste to me this evening, when I think that my contribution towards it, has obliged me to break my promise to this poor woman; and that it will cause her, for at least another week, to endure all the sufferings of exposure to cold without sufficient covering."

Henrietta Harwood, as leader of the conspiracy, was extremely busy every moment that she could snatch from the presence of Mrs. Middleton and the teachers, in making arrangements for the feast of the evening. There was a great deal of whispering and consulting, between her and the elder girls, as to what they should have; and a great deal of talking on the stairs to Mary the chambermaid; who, for the bribe of a quarter of a dollar, had consented to procure for them whatever they wished, without the knowledge of Mrs. Middleton. It was unanimously agreed that none of the *little* girls were to be let into the secret, as their discretion was not to be depended on; and there was much lamentation that the bed-hour for the children was so late as eight o'clock. The little girls all slept in one large room, and as soon as they had gone to be prepared for bed, under the superintendence of Mary, Henrietta proposed that herself and six other young ladies should volunteer to assist in undressing them. "You know," said she, "there are eight of the children, and if we each take a child and leave one to Mary, they can be got to bed in an eighth part of the time that it will require for Mary to attend to all of them herself. Just, you know, as they have quilting frolics and husking frolics in the country, when a whole week's work is accomplished in a few hours, by assembling a great many persons to join in it."

This proposal was immediately assented to; and a committee of half a dozen young ladies, with Henrietta at their head, adjourned to the children's apartment. "Come, little chits," said Henrietta, "as it is a cold night, we are going to have an undressing frolic, and to help Mary to put you all to bed: for the sooner you are tucked up in your nests the better it will be for you,—and for us too," she added in a low voice aside to Miss Thomson. "Here, Rosalie Sunbridge," she continued, "come to me, I will do the honours for *you*, as you are a sort of pet of mine."

The elder girls then began undressing the little ones with such violence that strings snapped, buttons were jerked off, and stockings torn in the process. The children wondered why the young ladies were seized with such a sudden and unusual fit of kindness, and why they went so energetically to work in getting them undressed and put to bed.

An altercation, however, ensued between Henrietta Harwood and Rosalie Sunbridge, who declared that it was her mother's particular desire that her hair behind should be curled in papers every night; a ceremony that Henrietta proposed omitting, telling her that there was already sufficient curl remaining in her hair to last all the next day, and reminding her that there was no such trouble with the hair of the other little girls. "That is becausethey have no hair to curl," replied Rosalie; "you know that they are all closely cropped. But if you will not roll up mine in papers, Miss Harwood, I would rather have Mary to put me to bed, though you *do* call me your pet." "Well, well, hush, and I *will* do it," said Henrietta; "but it shall be done in a new way which saves a great deal of trouble, and makes very handsome curls when the hair is opened out next morning." So saying, she snatched up a great piece of coarse brown paper, and seizing the little girl's hind hair in her hand, she rolled it all up in one large curl; Rosalie crying out at the violence with which she pulled, and the other children laughing, when it was done, at the huge knob, and telling Rosalie she had a knocker at her back.

In a short time the night-gowns and night-caps were scrambled on, and the children all deposited in their respective beds, and all hastily kissed by their undressers; who hurried out of the room, anxious to enter upon their anticipated delights.

"Now, good Mary, dear Mary," said Henrietta, "do tell me if you have got every thing?" "Every thing, miss," replied Mary, "except the calves-foot jelly; and the money fell short of that. But I have got the iced pound-cake, and the mince pies, and the oyster patties, and the little cocoa-nut puddings, and the bottle of lemon-syrup, and all the other things. They are snug and safe in the market-basket in the back-kitchen-closet; and nobody can never guess nothing about it."

Just at this moment the man-servant came to tell the young ladies that Mrs. Middleton wished them all to go down into the front parlour to look at some prints. These prints were the coloured engravings of Wall's beautiful views on the Hudson, and which had just been purchased by Mrs. Middleton's brother-in-law, who was going to leave the city the following morning. At any other time the young ladies (at least those who had a taste for drawing) would have been grateful for Mrs. Middleton's kindness in allowing them an opportunity of looking at these fine landscapes; but *now*every moment that detained them from the feast, seemed like an hour. Henrietta murmured almost aloud; and they all went down with reluctance, except Isabella Caldwell, who had made up her mind not to partake of the banquet.

In the mean time, little Rosalie Sunbridge, who was a very cunning child, and had a great deal of curiosity, suspected that something more than usual was going on, from the alertness of the young ladies in hurrying the children to bed. *Her* bed being nearest to the door, she had overheard the elder girls in earnest consultation with the chambermaid in the passage, and although she could not distinguish exactly what was said, she understood that something very delightful was to go on that evening in the front school-room. Having a great desire to know precisely what was in agitation, she waited a short time till all her companions were asleep; and then getting up softly, she opened one of the shutters to let in a little light, as the storm had subsided and there was a faint moon. She then got her merino coat, and put it on over her night-gown, and covering her feet with her carpet moccasins that she might make no noise in walking, she stole softly into the front school-room, determined to watch all that went on.

Two lamps were burning on the table; but no person was in the room; the young ladies having all gone down into the parlour to look at the prints. Rosalie, by climbing on a chair, managed, with much difficulty, to get on the upper shelf of a large closet; having hastily cleared a space for herself to lie down in, among the books and rolls of maps. Then pushing away the chair, she drew the closet-door nearly close; leaving only a small crack, through which she could observe all that was done.

Presently, she saw Mary come cautiously into the room with a basket, and taking out of it the materials for the feast, the girl arranged them all to great advantage on the table. When this was accomplished, she went down stairs; and immediately after, the young ladies, having looked hastily at the prints, all came up, and expressed much satisfaction at the inviting appearance of the banquet. Isabella lighted a small lamp, and said she was going to bed.

"Why, Caldwell," exclaimed Henrietta, "are you absolutely in earnest? What, after contributing to the expense of the feast, will you really leave us before it begins, and go dismally to bed? See how nice every thing looks."

"Every thing, indeed, looks nice," replied Isabella, "but still I have no desire to partake of them. I am out of spirits, and I have other reasons for not wishing to join your party." "Just take something before you go," said Henrietta. "No," answered Isabella, "I feel as if I could not taste a single article on the table."

She then withdrew to her room, and her companions took their seats and began to regale themselves; Henrietta presiding at the head of the table. They would have enjoyed their feast very much, only that, notwithstanding their expected security, they were in continual dread of being discovered. They started, and listened at every little noise; fearing that Miss Loxley might possibly have returned, or that Mrs. Middleton might possibly be coming up stairs.

"Really," said Henrietta, "it is a great pity that poor Isabella Caldwell, after she gave her dollar with so much reluctance, should refuse to take any share of our feast. Perhaps to-morrow she will think better of it. Suppose we save something for her. I dare say she will have no objection to eat some of these good things in the morning."

"Put by one of the little cocoa-nut puddings for her," said Miss Scott. "And one of the mince pies," said another young lady. "And a large slice of pound-cake," said a third. "And a bunch of white grapes," said a fourth.

Henrietta then selected some of the nicest articles of their banquet, to offer to Isabella in the morning; and after some consultation, it was concluded to deposit them, for the present, in the farthest corner of the upper shelf of the closet; which upper shelf was only used as a repository for old maps and old copy books, and waste paper, and with these the things could be very conveniently covered. "Do not take a light to the closet," said Miss Marley, "you may set something on fire. If you stand on tiptoe and raise your arm as high as you can, you may easily reach the upper shelf."

Henrietta accordingly walked to the closet; and was in the act of shoving a mince-pie into a dark corner of the upper shelf, when suddenly she gave a start and a shriek, and let fall the cocoa-nut pudding which she held in her hand. "What is the matter?" exclaimed all the girls at once. "Oh!" cried Henrietta, "when I reached up the mince-pie to the top shelf, it was taken from me by a cold hand that met mine—I felt the fingers." "Impossible," said some of the girls. "What could it actually be?" cried others. Just then, Rosalie made a rustling among the loose papers on the top shelf. "There it is again," screamed Henrietta. "Oh!" cried Miss Watkins, "we have done very wrong to plot this feast in secret, and something dreadful is going to happen to us as a punishment."

Another rustling set all the young ladies to screaming; and, with one accord, they rushed towards the door, with such force as to overset the table and all its contents. The lamps were broken and extinguished in the fall; several of the girls were thrown down by the others; and the shrieks were so violent that Mrs. Middleton heard them into the parlour, where, her friends having left her, she was sitting with Miss Loxley, who had just come in; and taking a light with them, the two ladies ran up to the front school-room.

The scene which then presented itself transfixed them with astonishment. The floor was strewed with the remains of the feast. The oil from the shattered lamps was running among the cakes and pies, which were also drenched with water from a broken pitcher; near which the bottle of lemon-syrup was lying in fragments. The table was thrown down on its side. Some of the young ladies were still prostrate on the floor, and all were screaming. Rosalie (frightened at the uproar she had caused) was on her hands and knees, looking out from the upper shelf of the closet, and crying"O, take me down, take me down! somebody bring a chair and take me down."

Isabella Caldwell, hearing the noise, had thrown on her flannel gown, and ran also to see what was the matter. As soon as the surprise of Mrs. Middleton would allow her to speak, she inquired the cause of all this disturbance; but she could get no other answer than that there was some horrible thing in the closet. "There is indeed something in the closet," said Mrs. Middleton, perceiving Rosalie. "Miss Sunbridge, how came you up there, and in that dress? and what is the meaning of all this?"

The young ladies, having recovered from their terror when they found it to be groundless, and Miss Loxley having taken down Rosalie, Henrietta made a candid confession of the whole business. Acknowledging herself to be the proposer and leader of the plot, she expressed her readiness to submit to any punishment Mrs. Middleton might think proper to inflict on her, but hoped that her governess would have the goodness to pardon all the other young ladies; none of whom would have thought of a secret feast, if she had not suggested it to them. "Above all," continued Henrietta, "I must exculpate Isabella Caldwell, who declined going to table with us or partaking of any thing, but retired to her bed; as may be known by her being now in her night-clothes."

Mrs. Middleton was touched with the generosity of Henrietta Harwood, in taking all the blame on herself to exonerate her companions; and as her kind heart would not allow her to send any of her pupils to bed in the anticipation of being punished the next day, she said, "Miss Harwood, I will for this time permit your misdemeanour to go unpunished, but I require a promise from you that it shall never be repeated. Make that promise sincerely, and I feel assured that you will keep it."

"O, yes, indeed, dear madam!" sobbed Henrietta, "you are too kind; and I cannot forgive myself for having persuaded my companions to join in a plot which I knew you would disapprove."

"Go now to your beds," said Mrs. Middleton, "and I will send a servant to clear away the disorder of this room. Rosalie, I see, has already slipped off to hers."

Next morning, before school commenced, Mrs. Middleton addressed the young ladies mildly but impressively, on the proceedings of the day before. She dwelt on the general impropriety of all secret contrivances; on the injury done to the integrity of the ignorant servant-girl, by bribing her to deceive her employer; on the danger of making themselves sick by eating such a variety of sweet things; and on the folly of expending in those dainties, money which might be much better employed.

"That," said Henrietta, "was one of Isabella Caldwell's objections to joining our feasting party. I am now convinced that she had in view some more sensible manner of disposing of her money. I regret that she was prevailed on to contribute her dollar, as she must have had an excellent reason for her unwillingness; and she seemed really unhappy, and went to bed without touching any of our good things."

"I can guess how it was," said Miss Loxley. "One very cold morning last week, I met Diana, Miss Caldwell's washerwoman, going up stairs with the clean clothes, and having nothing on her shoulders but an old cotton shawl. I asked her if she had no cloak, and she replied that she had not; but added, that Miss Isabella had been so kind as to promise her one, which was to be ready for her when she came again. I suspect that Miss Caldwell has been saving her money for the laudable purpose of furnishing this poor woman with a cloak."

"Oh! no doubt she has," exclaimed Henrietta. "Why, dear Isabella, did you not say so? and bad as I am, I would not have persisted in persuading you out of your dollar."

"The woman, however, did not get her cloak," resumed Miss Loxley, "for I again saw her without one, yesterday, though the weather had increased in severity."

"It is true," said Isabella. "The cloak was to have cost four dollars, and after subscribing one dollar to the feast, I could not buy it; as I had not then sufficient money."

Mrs. Middleton. Miss Harwood, had you often these feasts at Madame Disette's.

Henrietta. Oh! very often, and as the teacher, Miss Benson, was always one of the party, we managed so well, that Madame Disette never discovered us. Or if she had any suspicion, she said nothing about it; for after all, she cared very little what we did out of school-hours provided that our proceedings *cost her nothing.*

Mrs. Middleton. You must not speak so disrespectfully of your former governess. But I will explain to you that *I* care very much what you do, even in your hours of recreation. It is when the business of the school is over, and they are no longer in the presence of their instructors, that girls are in the greatest danger of forming bad habits, and imitating bad examples. All deceit, all tricks, are highly unjustifiable. A little feast may seem in itself of small moment; but if you persist in plotting little feasts, you will eventually be led on to plot things of more importance, and which may lead to the worst consequences. Then, as I always allow you as large a portion of sweet things as comports with your health, it is the more reprehensible in you to seek to procure them for yourselves, without my knowledge. Tell me now, do any of you feel the better for last night's frolic?

Miss Thomson. O, no, no! Miss Watkins and Miss Roberts were sick all night; and, indeed, none of us feel very well this morning.

Mrs. Middleton. I observed that you all had very little appetite for your breakfast.

Miss Brownlow. And then *I* had my new frock spoiled when I fell down in the lamp-oil.

Miss Wilcox. And I got some lamp-oil into my mouth. I tasted it all night. Even my nose was rubbed in it, as I lay struggling on the floor.

Miss Snodgrass. And *I* fell with my knees on half a dozen pieces of orange, and stained my black silk frock, so that it is no longer fit to wear.

Miss Marley. And *I* was thrown down with the back of my head on a bunch of grapes, mashing them to a jelly.

Miss Scott. But *my* hair was so very sticky, with falling into the lemon syrup, that I was obliged, this morning, to wash it all over with warm soap-suds.

Miss Roberts. And *I* put my foot into the bottom of the broken pitcher, and cut my heel so that it bled through the stocking.

Miss Watkins. Still, nothing of this would have happened if Rosalie Sunbridge had stayed in her bed. It was her hiding in the closet and frightening us, that caused all the mischief.

Rosalie. I am sure I was punished enough for my curiosity; for when I got on the closet-shelf I was obliged to lie so cramped that I was almost stiff; and I was half dead with cold, notwithstanding I had put on my merino coat. And then I was longing all the time for some of the good things I saw you eating; so that when Miss Harwood came to hide the mince-pie, I could not forbear taking it out of her hand. When I found that you were all so terrified, I thought I would make a noise among the loose papers to frighten you still more, supposing that you would all quit the room; and that then I could come down from the shelf, and regale myself awhile, before I stole back to-bed. I did not foresee that you would overset the table in your flight, and make such a violent noise. But I will never again attempt to pry into other people's secrets.

Mrs Middleton. I hope you never will. This feast, you see, has caused nothing but discomfort, which is the case with all things that are in themselves improper. Yet I think the greatest sufferer is Isabella Caldwell's washerwoman, who has, in consequence, been disappointed of her cloak.

Isabella. Next week, madam, when I receive my allowance, I hope to be able to buy it for her.

Mrs. Middleton. You need not wait till next week. The poor woman shall suffer no longer for a cloak. Here is a dollar in advance; and after school, you can go out and purchase it, so that it may be ready for her to-morrow when she brings home your clothes.

Isabella. Dear Mrs. Middleton, how much I thank you.

The young ladies having promised that they would attempt no more private feasts, Mrs. Middleton kissed, and forgave them. After school, Isabella, accompanied by Miss Loxley, went out and bought the plaid cloak, which was sent home directly. Next day, she longed for Diana to arrive with the clothes, that she might enjoy her pleasure on receiving so useful a gift, but, to her great disappointment they were brought home by another mulatto woman, who informed Isabella that she was Diana's next door neighbour, and that poor Diana having taken a violent cold from being out in the snow-storm, was now confined to her bed with the rheumatism. "Ah!" thought Isabella, "perhaps if she had had this good warm cloak to go home in, the day before yesterday, she might have escaped the rheumatism. I see now that whenever we allow ourselves to be persuaded to do a thingwhich we know to be wrong, evil is sure to come from it."

She desired the woman to wait a few minutes; and hastening to Mrs. Middleton, begged that she would allow her to go and see poor Diana, who, she feared was in great distress. Mrs. Middleton readily consented, and had a basket filled with various things, which she gave to the woman to carry with the plaid cloak to Diana. She sent by Isabella a bottle of camphor, and some cotton wadding, for Diana's rheumatism, and a medicine for her to take internally. Miss Loxley accompanied Isabella; and they found Diana in bed and very ill, and every thing about her evincing extreme poverty. Isabella engaged the woman to stay with Diana till she got well, and to take care of her and her children, promising to pay her for her trouble. When they returned and made their report to Mrs. Middleton, she wrote a note to her physician, requesting him to visit Diana and attend her as long as was necessary.

Next week, Henrietta Harwood, and the other young ladies, subscribed all their allowance of pocket-money for the relief of Diana; who very soon was well enough to resume her work. It is unnecessary to add that their contribution to the support of the poor woman and her family, gave them far more pleasure than they had derived from the unfortunate feast. They never, of course, attempted another. And Henrietta Harwood, at Mrs. Middleton's school, lost all the faults she had acquired at Madame Disette's.

THE WEEK OF IDLENESS.

"Their only labour was to kill the time,And labour dire it was, and weary wo."

A delaide and Rosalind, the daughters of Mr. Edington, looked forward with much pleasure to the arrival of their cousin, Josephine Sherborough, from Maryland. She was to spend the summer with them, at their father's country residence on the beautiful bay of New York, a few miles below the city; and, though they had never seen her, they were disposed to regard Josephine as a very agreeable addition to their family society. Having had the misfortune to lose their mother, Adelaide and Rosalind had been for several years under the entire care of their governess, Mrs. Mortlake; a highly accomplished and most amiable woman, whom they loved and respected as if she had been their parent, and by whose instructions they had greatly profited.

It was on a beautiful evening in June, that Josephine Sherborough was *certainly* expected, after several disappointments within the last two or three weeks. The Miss Edingtons and their governess were seated on one of the settees in the portico that extended along the front of Mr. Edington's house. Mrs. Mortlake was sewing, Rosalind reading aloud, and Adelaide, with her drawing materials before her, was earnestly engaged in colouring a sketch of a fishing-boat at anchor, beautifully reflected in the calm water, and tinted with the glowing rays of the declining sun. As she put in the last touches, she hoped, before the summer was over, that she should improve so much in her drawing as to be enabled to attempt a view of the bay with its green shores; its island fortresses; and its numerous ships, some going out on a voyage to distant regions, others coming home with the merchandise and the news of Europe.

"Now," exclaimed Adelaide, "I see the smoke of the steamboat, just behind Castle Williams. My father and Josephine will soon be here. I am glad my drawing is so nearly completed. In a few minutes it will be finished."

"And in a few minutes," said Rosalind, "I shall conclude the story that I am reading."

"Do you not now think," asked Mrs. Mortlake, "I was right in proposing that we should protract our usual afternoon occupations an hour beyond the usual time, as we are expecting the arrival of your father and your cousin? This last hour would have seemed twice its real length, if we had done nothing, all the while, but strain our eyes in gazing up the bay for the steamboat, saying every few minutes, 'Oh, I wish they were come!'"

In a short time, Adelaide exclaimed, "Here is the steamboat. I see they are depositing several trunks in the little boat at the side. And now it is let down to the water. And now a gentleman and a young lady descend the steps, and take their seats in it. How fast it cuts its way through the foam that is raised by the tow-line. In a moment it will touch the wharf. Here they come. There is my father; and it *must* be Josephine that is with him!"

The sisters then ran down the steps of the portico, and in a moment were at the landing-place, where Mr. Edington, as soon as he had assisted her to step on shore, introduced them to Josephine Sherborough, a fat, fair, pale young lady, about fourteen, with a remarkably placid countenance which immediately won the regard of Rosalind: who determined in her own mind that Josephine was a very sweet girl, and that they should, ever hereafter, be intimate and most particular friends. Adelaide, who was two years older than Rosalind, and who had more penetration, was not so violently prepossessed in favour of her cousin, whose face she thought deficient in animation, and whose movements were more slow and heavy than those of any young girl she had ever seen.

When tea was over, the sisters proposed to Josephine a walk round the garden, which was large and very beautiful; but she complained of being excessively tired, and said that she would much rather go to bed. This somewhat surprised her cousins, as they knew that Josephine had been three days in the city with the friends under whose care she had come from Maryland; and they thought that she must have had ample time to recover from the fatigue of her journey: to which her last little trip in the steamboat could not have added much. Rosalind, who was a year younger than Josephine, accompanied her to the chamber prepared for her accommodation, where Josephine, looking round disconsolately, inquired if there was no servant to undress her. Rosalind volunteered to perform this office; and Josephine said she would ring the bell for one of the maids, when she wished to get up in the morning.

She kept the family waiting breakfast for her till nine o'clock, and then came down in a white slip or loose gown; her hair still pinned up; her eyes half shut; and her face evidently not washed. Mr. Edington, whose business in the city made it necessary for him to be there at an early hour, had long since breakfasted, and gone up to town in the boat; and after a few days, the rest of the family ceased to wait for her; and the housekeeper was directed to have a fresh breakfast prepared for Miss Sherborough whenever she came down.

The first days of Josephine's visit ought, in Rosalind's opinion, to have been devoted entirely to the amusement of their guest, and she was urgent with Mrs. Mortlake, to allow Adelaide and herself a week of holiday. Their governess told them that she would have been willing to grant this indulgence if Josephine was to remain with them a week only: but as she was to stay all summer, it would, of course, be impossible for them, every day, to give up their usual occupations; and therefore it was better to begin as they were to go on. She reminded Rosalind that if they were attentive and industrious, they would get through their lessons the sooner, and have the more time for recreation with their visitor.

After Josephine had breakfasted, Mrs. Mortlake offered to show her the children's library, that she might amuse herself with any of the books she chose, while her cousins were engaged in their morning employments. Josephine thanked her; but said she could entertain herself very well without books, and that she believed she would take a walk in the garden. She accordingly put on her bonnet, and strolled up and down the walks, gazing listlessly at the flowers. She attempted to gather some strawberries, but found it too fatiguing to stoop down to the beds; and satisfied herself with plucking currants and gooseberries from the bushes. She then sat in the arbour for awhile, and looked all the time straight down the middle walk. When she was tired of the arbour, she established herself on a circular bench which ran round a large walnut tree; and then she counted all thewindows at sat the back part of the house. When this was accomplished, she counted them all over again. And then, finding the sun had become very powerful, she went into the front-parlour, the shutters of which were bowed to exclude the heat, and throwing herself at full length on the sofa, she in a few minutes fell into a profound sleep, from which she did not awaken till her cousins entered the room in search of her, after their lessons were over. They took her up stairs into the apartment they called their play-room, and showed her a variety of things which would have been very amusing to a girl that knew how to be amused. There was a lacquered Chinese cabinet, containing a great number of curiosities brought by their uncle from Canton: and a large box with shelves, on which were various specimens of Indian ingenuity, presented to the children by a gentleman who had travelled all over the country beyond the Mississippi. Their library consisted of a beautiful and entertaining selection of juvenile books; and they had a port-folio filled with fine prints of such subjects as are particularly interesting to young people. They showed her a representation of the grand procession at the coronation of the sovereign of England, printed on a long narrow roll of paper pasted on silk; which paper was unwound like a ribbon-yard from a Tunbridge-ware box, and it could be screwed up again after being sufficiently seen. It was many yards in length, and the figures (which were almost innumerable) were elegantly designed, and beautifully coloured. They had also a little theatre, with a great number of scenes; and a variety of very small dolls, dressed in appropriate habits to personate the actors. Beside all these things, they had a closet full of amusing toys; and in short the play-room was amply stored with a profusion of whatever was necessary to the enjoyment of their leisure hours.

But all was lost on Josephine. While Adelaide and Rosalind were assiduous in showing and explaining to her every thing, she heard them with listlessness and apathy, and made not the slightest remark. At last, she said "We will reserve some of these sights for to-morrow. I must go and dress myself for dinner. Oh! how I hate to dress. It is an odious task. I must have Mary to assist me again; for I never *can* get through the fatigue of dressing myself, and fixing my hair."

In the afternoon, Adelaide and Rosalind took their sewing, and seated themselves with Mrs. Mortlake in the porch. As Josephine appeared to have no work, Mrs. Mortlake gave her a volume of Miss Edgeworth's Moral Tales, and requested her to read one of them aloud. Josephine took the book and began to read "The Prussian Vase," but with so monotonous and inarticulate a tone, or rather drawl, that it was painful to hear her: and her cousins were not sorry when, at the end of three or four pages, she stopped, and complained that she was too much fatigued to read any more.

Mrs. Mortlake then desired Adelaide, who read extremely well, to take the book and continue the story, but in a short time Josephine was discovered to be asleep. When Adelaide ceased reading, Josephine awoke, and saying that she could not live without her afternoon nap, went up stairs to lie down on her bed.

She slept till near tea-time, and when tea was over, her cousins and Mrs. Mortlake prepared for a walk, and invited Josephine to join them. This she did; but in less than ten minutes she complained so much of fatigue, that Rosalind turned back and accompanied her home, and she reclined on the settee in the porch till the lamps were lighted in the front-parlour. The girls then showed Josephine a portable diorama, containing twelve beautiful coloured views of castles, abbeys, temples, and mountain scenery. Each of these exquisite little landscapes was fixed, in turn, as the back scene of a sort of miniature stage. The skies and lights of these views were all transparent, and there were other skies which turned on rollers, and represented sunrise, moonlight, sunshine, and thunder-clouds. These second skies being placed behind those of the picture, were slowly unrolled by turning a small handle, and produced the most varied and beautiful effects on the scenery, which could thus at pleasure be illuminated gradually with sunshine or moonbeams, or darkened with the clouds of a gathering storm. But Josephine saw this charming exhibition without a single comment; being evidently much inclined to yawn as she looked at it. And getting again very sleepy, she soon retired to her bed.

Next morning, Mrs. Mortlake invited her to bring her sewing into the school-room, and sit there while her cousins were at their lessons. But Josephine replied that she hated sewing, and never did any. However, she took her seat in the school-room, and a kitten soon after came purring round her; so she put it on her lap, and stroked and patted it till the lessons were over, and the girls went up stairs to amuse themselves till dinner-time.

Adelaide tried to induce Josephine to look at some of the beautiful prints in the port-folio; but she found it necessary to explain them all, as if she was showing them to a child of three years old.

Rosalind proposed that they should all go on the roof of the house (it being flat on the top and guarded with a railing) to look at the beauty and wide extent of the prospect; and taking their parasols to screen their heads from the sun, they went up through a very convenient trap-door at the head of an easy little staircase. The view from the roof of Mr. Edington's house was certainly very fine, comprising the bay with its islands and fortresses; its boats and vessels of every description; the distant lighthouse at Sandy Hook, and the blue ocean rolling beyond it: and at the other end of the scene, behind a forest of masts, rose the city of New York with its numerous spires glittering in the sunlight.

Fine as the prospect was, Josephine showed no symptom of admiration; but as they came down through the garret-passage, she spied an old rocking-chair standing in a corner among some lumber. (Parlour rocking-chairs were not yet in general use.) She turned her head, and looked at it with longing eyes. "Ah!" said she, "that is the very thing I have been suffering for ever since I left home. Do let me beg to have it in my room." The chair, accordingly, was carried into the apartment of Josephine, who immediately seated herself, and began to rock with great satisfaction; at which most interesting amusement she continued till near dinner-time. The rocking-chair was next day taken into the school-room, and with that and the kitten, Josephine appeared to get through the morning rather contentedly.

The afternoon was again devoted to a long nap: and in the evening Josephine reclined on the front-parlour sofa, and entertained herself by running her finger a hundred times over the brass nails.

Several days passed on in a similar manner. One morning when they were all in the play-room, Josephine said to her cousins, "What a very hard life you are obliged to endure. Neither of you have a moment of rest, from the time you leave your beds in the morning, till you return to them at night. First, there is your rising with the sun, and going to work in your little gardens. I am sure you might make your father's gardener do all that business."

Adelaide. But we take great pleasure in it; and when we see our flowers growing and blooming, the interest they excite in us is much increased by knowing that we have raised them from the seed, or planted the roots ourselves; and that we have assisted their growth by watering, weeding, tying them, and clearing them from insects. And is it not pleasant to find that the fruit-stones, we planted a few years since in our little orchard, have produced trees that are now loaded with fruit? The red cherries, we had last evening after tea, were from one of my trees; and the large black cherries were from Rosalind's. And in August, we shall have our own plums and peaches.

Josephine. I am sure it is much less trouble to buy these things, than to cultivate them; and as to the amusement, I can see none. Then there are those awful lessons that are always to come on after breakfast. The writing, and cyphering, and grammar, and geography, and history, one day: and the French, and music, and drawing, the next: and-the reading and sewing every afternoon; and the walk every evening. Even your play-time (as you call it) is a time of perpetual fatigue: your plays all seem to require so much skill and ingenuity. And then on Saturday morning, to think that you are obliged to go into the housekeeper's room and learn to make cakes, and pastry, and sweetmeats, and all such things. I am sure if I was never to eat cakes till I assisted in making them, I should go without all my life. It seems to me that your whole existence is a course of uninterrupted toil.

Rosalind. There is much truth in what you say, my dear Josephine. But I own it never struck me before.

Adelaide. We have always been perfectly happy in our occupations and amusements: and the longest day in summer seems too short for us.

Josephine. Too short, perhaps, to get through such a quantity of work; for I consider all this as *real hard work.* I am glad that I have not been brought up in such a laborious manner. My parents love me too much to make me uncomfortable, even for a moment; or to cause me in any way the slightest fatigue. I have spent my whole life in ease and peace; doing nothing but what I pleased, and never learning but when I chose. I have not been troubled with either a school or a governess; my mother (who was herself educated at a boarding-school) having determined, as I was her only child, to instruct me at home.

Adelaide saw that it was in vain to argue the point any farther. But the foolish reasoning of Josephine made a great impression on Rosalind; so true it is, that "evil communication corrupts good manners," and she was seized with an earnest desire to participate in the happiness of doing nothing.

Next morning, Rosalind went to her lessons with great reluctance, and consequently did not perform them well. On the following day she was equally deficient; and in the afternoon when Josephine went up stairs to take her nap, Rosalind, looking after her, exclaimed, "Happy girl! How I envy her!"

"Envy her!" said Adelaide, "of all the people I am acquainted with, I think Josephine Sherborough is the least to be envied."

Rosalind. She is not troubled with lessons, and sewing, as we are. She can do whatever she pleases the whole day long. No wonder she is fat, when she is so perfectly comfortable. For my part, I expect, in the course of another year, to be worn to a skeleton with such incessant application.

Adelaide. But without application how is it possible to learn?

Rosalind. I would rather put off my learning till I am older, and have strength to bear such dreadful fatigue.

Adelaide. I do not find it fatiguing. I am sure our lessons are not very long, and Mrs. Mortlake is so kind and gentle, that it is a pleasure to be instructed by her; and she explains every thing so sensibly and intelligibly.

Rosalind. But where is the use of learning every thing before we grow up?

Adelaide. Because, as Mrs. Mortlake says, children (if they are not *too young*) learn faster than grown persons; their memories are better, as they have not yet been overloaded, and they have nothing of importance to divert their attention from their lessons.

Rosalind. I would rather grow up as ignorant as our tenant's wife, Dutch Katy, than be made such a slave as I am now. I am sure Katy's life is an easy one compared to mine.

Adelaide, smiling. Consider it not so deeply.

Rosalind. Yes, I will, for I am out of patience. I wish it was the fashion to be ignorant.

Adelaide. Fortunately it is *not*. To say nothing of the disgrace of being ignorant when it is known we have had opportunities of acquiring knowledge, persons whose minds are vacant, have but few enjoyments. For instance, as Josephine knows nothing of music, it gives her no pleasure to hear the finest singing and playing, even such as Mrs. Mortlake's. As she has no idea of drawing, she takes not the least delight in looking at beautiful pictures. Having never been in the habit of reading, she wonders how it is possible to be amused with a book; and as she has no knowledge of history or geography, she often, when she *does* read, is puzzled with allusions to those subjects; and a French word is as unintelligible to her, as if it were Greek. Plants and animals do not interest her, because she has scarcely an idea of the properties or attributes of any of the productions of Nature. And what is worse than all, she takes no pleasure in listening to the conversation of sensible people, because she is incapable of understanding it: her comprehension being only equal to the most frivolous topics.

Rosalind. Notwithstanding all this, her life passes calmly and pleasantly; and I am sure she is much happier than we are.

Adelaide. Speak for yourself, dear Rosalind. For my part, I do not wish to be more happy than I am.

Rosalind. Well, I thought so too, till I knew Josephine. And she is by no means so dull as you suppose.

Adelaide. Perhaps she is not naturally stupid; but indulgence and indolence have so benumbed her understanding, that it seems now incapable of the smallest effort.

At this moment Mrs. Mortlake came down with a book in her hand, for the afternoon reading.

"Rosalind," said she, "as my room is over the porch, and the windows are open, I could not avoid hearing all you have just been saying, particularly as you spoke very loudly. As I do not wish to see either of my pupils *unhappy*, I will gratify your desire, and both you and Adelaide (if it is also her wish) may pass a week entirely without occupation; in short, a week of idleness."

Adelaide. O no, dear Mrs. Mortlake: I have no desire to avail myself of your offer. I would much rather continue my usual employments.

Rosalind. A week of entire leisure! O, how delightful!

Mrs. Mortlake. But, during that time, neither you nor Josephine must come into the school-room.

Rosalind. O, indeed! we shall not desire it.

Mrs. Mortlake. Neither must you read.

Rosalind. Well!—I am sure I have read enough to last my lifetime. Where is the use of reading story-books that are all invention, describing people that never lived; or of poring over voyages and travels to countries I shall never visit; or of studying the histories of dead kings.

Mrs. Mortlake. You must not sew.

Rosalind. I never *did* find it very entertaining to stick a needle and thread into a piece of muslin, and pull it through again.

Mrs. Mortlake. You must not draw.

Rosalind. I do not see the pleasure of rubbing red, and blue, and green paint on little plates; and dabbling in tumblers of water with camel's-hair pencils, and daubing colours on white paper.

Mrs. Mortlake. You must not play on the piano, nor on the harp.

Rosalind. Well! What sense is there in pressing down your fingers first on bits of ivory, and then on bits of ebony; and staring at crotchets and quavers all the time? or where is the use of twanging and jerking the strings of a harp?

Mrs. Mortlake. You must not work in your garden.

Rosalind. So much the better. Then I shall neither dirty my hands with pulling up the weeds, nor splash my feet with the water-pot.

Mrs. Mortlake. You may sleep as much as you please; but you must not rise before nine o'clock.

Rosalind. O, how delightful, not to be obliged to jump out of bed at daylight! Dearest Mrs. Mortlake, if I could have a *month* of ease and comfort, instead of only a week—-

Mrs. Mortlake. Well,—if at the end of the week you still desire it, perhaps I may protract the indulgence to a longer period.

Rosalind. Dear Mrs. Mortlake, how kind you are. When shall my happiness begin? As to-morrow is Saturday, when we *always* have a half holiday, and next day Sunday, when we go to the city to attend church, I think, notwithstanding my impatience, I would rather commence my week of felicity regularly on Monday morning.

Mrs. Mortlake. Very well, then. On Monday morning let it be.

Adelaide. I am sorry to hear you call your anticipated week of idleness a week of felicity.

Rosalind. Oh! I am sure I shall find it so; and you will regret not having also accepted Mrs. Mortlake's kind offer.

Adelaide. I fear no regret on that subject.

Mrs. Mortlake. Say no more, Adelaide. Wait till we see the event of Rosalind's experiment.

Rosalind. I hope Josephine's afternoon nap will not be as long as usual: I am so impatient to tell her. O, how we shall enjoy ourselves together!

When Josephine awoke and heard of the new arrangement, she was as much delighted as *she* could be at any thing; and she begged that Rosalind might be allowed to share her chamber during this happy week.

Monday morning came; and Rosalind (such is the power of habit) awoke, as usual, with the dawn; but soon recollected that she was not to get up till nine o'clock. She saw the light gleaming through the Venetian shutters, and she heard the morning song of the scarlet oriole, whose nest was in a locust tree close to the window; and the twittering of the martins as they flew about their box, which was affixed to the wall just below the roof of the house. She heard Adelaide, who was in the next room, get up to dress herself, and exclaim as she threw open the shutters, "O, what a beautiful sunrise!" Rosalind felt some desire to enjoy the loveliness of the early morning; but determined to remain in bed, and indulge herself with another nap. She turned and shook her pillow, and tumbled about for a long time before she could get to sleep; and at last she awoke again just as the clock was striking seven. She had still two hours to remain in bed, and she found the time extremely tedious. "Are you asleep, Josephine?" said she. "No," replied Josephine, "I am never asleep after this hour."

Rosalind. Why, then, do you remain in bed?

Josephine. O, because I hate to get up.

Rosalind. Well then let us talk.

Josephine. O, no! I never talk in bed. For, even when I do not sleep, I am not quite awake.

At length it was nine; and at the first stroke of the clock, Rosalind started from her bed, and began to wash and dress herself. When the girls went down stairs, they found the family breakfast had long been over, and they had theirs on a little table in a corner of the room. Rosalind thought her breakfast did not taste very well; probably, because remaining so long in bed, had taken away her appetite.

After breakfast, they went out and walked a little while in the most shady part of the garden. Then they sat down; first in the arbour of honeysuckles, then on the green bank behind the ice-house; then on a garden chair; and then on the bench at the foot of the great walnut tree. They picked a few currants and ate them; and they gathered some roses and smelled them. For some time they held their parasols over their heads; and then they shut them, and made marks on the gravel with the ends of the ivory sticks. They looked awhile at a nursery of young peach-trees at one side of the garden; and then they turned and looked towards a clover-field on the other side. Josephine pulled the strings of her reticule backwards and forwards; and Rosalind counted the palisades in the fence of the kitchen-garden. At last a bright idea struck her; and she gathered some dandelions that were going to seed, and blew off the down; recommending the same amusement to Josephine, who, after two or three trials, gave it up.

"Suppose we go to the play-room," said Rosalind. Josephine assented, and they slowly walked back to the house, and ascended the stairs. "Now," said Rosalind, "we can play domino *in the morning.* Generally, we never amuse ourselves with any of those little games in the day-time; though we have domino, draughts, and loto, sometimes in the evening." They played domino awhile in a very spiritless manner, and then they tried draughts and loto, which they also soon gave up; Josephine saying that all these games required too much attention. She then had recourse to the rocking-chair, and Rosalind took some white paper and cut fly-traps; in which amusements they tried to get rid of the time till near the dinner-hour, when they combed their hair, and changed their dresses. Adelaide did not join them in the play-room, being much engaged with a very amusing book.

After dinner, Rosalind, accompanied Josephine to her room to take a nap likewise. But she found it so warm, and turned and tossed about so much, and had such difficulty in fixing herself in a comfortable position, that she thought, if it was not for the name of taking a nap, she had better have stayed up as usual. Josephine had less difficulty, being accustomed to afternoon-sleeping; and at length Rosalind shut her eyes, and fell into a sort of uneasy doze.

When they awoke, Rosalind proposed that they should put on their frocks, and go down into the porch, where Mrs. Mortlake and Adelaide were reading and sewing. But Josephine thought it would be much less trouble to sit in their loose gowns until near tea-time. To this Rosalind agreed, and they sat and gazed at the river. But it happened *this* afternoon that no ships came in, and only one went out; and all the steamboats kept far over towards the opposite shore. They were glad when the bell rung for tea; for when people do nothing, their meals are a sort of amusement, and are therefore expected with anxious interest. In the evening, they declined joining Mrs. Mortlake and Adelaide in their usual long walk, and took a short stroll under the willows on the bank of the river; after which they returned to the parlour, where Mr. Edington sat reading the newspaper, and Josephine threw herself on the sofa; while Rosalind sat beside her on a chair, and played with the kitten.

Next morning, their amusements in the garden were a little diversified by playing jack-stones and platting ribbon-grass; and when they went up to the play-room, Rosalind, looking among her old toys, found a doll long since laid aside, and a basket with its clothes. She offered the doll to Josephine proposing that she should dress it: but Josephine said "I would rather look at you, while *you* do it." Rosalind accordingly dressed the doll in two different suits, one after another; but soon grew tired, and had recourse to an ivory cup and ball, which she failed to catch with as much dexterity as usual. She gave Josephine a wooden lemon, which on being opened in the middle, contained a number of other lemons one within another, and diminishing in size till the last and smallest was no bigger than a pea. When Josephine had got through the lemon, Rosalind took it, and resigned the cup and ball to her cousin, who soon gave it up, as she could never make the cup catch the ball; and she again finished the morning with her never-failing resource the rocking-chair.

Monday, Tuesday, and Wednesday having been passed in this manner, on Thursday Rosalind began to acknowledge to herself, what she had indeed suspected on the first day, that a life of entire idleness was not quite so agreeable as she had supposed. Having no useful or interesting occupation to diversify her time, she found that play had lost its relish; and now that she could play all day, she found all plays tiresome. These three days had appeared to her of never-ending length; and she began to think that when her week of idleness had expired she would not solicit Mrs. Mortlake to prolong the term.

On Thursday afternoon Rosalind gave up her nap, and went and seated herself at the open window, that she might hear Mrs. Mortlake and Adelaide read aloud in the porch. And next morning, she actually stopped and listened at the school-room door while Adelaide was repeating her French lesson; and she returned again, and stood behind the door, to hear Mrs. Mortlake instructing her sister in a new song accompanied on the harp. All that day and the next, she felt as if she was actually sick of doing nothing; and she absolutely languished to be allowed once more to take a book and read, or to draw, or play on the piano. Even sewing, she thought, would now seem delightful to her.

On Saturday morning Rosalind met Adelaide in her brown linen apron with long sleeves, going into the housekeeper's room to assist in making cakes and pastry. She longed to go in with her, and to do her part as formerly; and her longing increased when she heard the sound of beating eggs, and grinding spice. She had hitherto looked forward with great pleasure to her holiday on Saturday afternoon. Now, after doing nothing all the week, Saturday afternoon had no charms for her; and she was glad to find it was to be devoted to a ride in the carriage, through a pleasant part of the adjacent country.

"Well, Rosalind," said Josephine, as they were taking off their bonnets, after their return from the ride, "you have now spent a week in *my* way. Do you not wish you could pass your whole life in the same manner?"

Rosalind. No, indeed—nor even another week. This week of idleness has seemed to me like a month; and I have no desire to renew the experiment. I have never in my life gone to bed so tired as after those days of doing nothing. I find that want of occupation is to me absolute misery; though it may be very delightful to *you*, as you have been brought up in a different manner, and have never been accustomed to any sort of employment. Yet, still I think you would be much happier, if you had something to do.

In the evening Mr. Edington said to his youngest daughter, "Well, Rosalind, how do you like your week of idleness? Are you going to request Mrs. Mortlake to lengthen the term of your enjoyment?"

Rosalind. O no, dear father; it has been no enjoyment to *me*. On the contrary, I am glad to think that it is now over. I have found it absolutely a punishment.

Mr. Edington. So I suspected.

Rosalind. And I deserved it, for allowing myself to become dissatisfied with the manner in which Mrs. Mortlake chose that I should occupy myself. I am tired of lying in bed, tired of idleness, and tired of play. So, dear Mrs. Mortlake, be so kind as to let me rise at daylight on Monday morning, to work in my garden, and resume my lessons as usual. You may depend on it I shall never again wish for a single day of idleness.

Mrs. Mortlake. I am very glad to hear you say so, my dear Rosalind. And I do not despair of at length convincing Josephine that she would be more happy if she had some regular employment.

That night Rosalind returned to her own chamber, and next morning she was up at daylight. It being Sunday, they went as usual to church in the city, and Rosalind was now delighted to pass the remainder of the day in reading a volume of Mrs. Sherwood's excellent work, the Lady of the Manor. A book now seemed like a novelty to her.

Next day Rosalind went through her lessons with a pleasure she had never felt before; and when they were over, she highly enjoyed her two hours' recreation after dinner. She took no more afternoon naps; and after a short time even Josephine was persuaded to give them up, and found it possible, with some practice, to keep awake while her cousins or Mrs. Mortlake were reading aloud in the porch.

Finally, Josephine became ashamed of being the only idle person in Mr. Edington's house, and was prevailed on by her uncle and Mrs. Mortlake to join her cousins in their lessons. By degrees, and by giving her only a very little to learn at a time, and by having constantly before her such good examples as Adelaide and Rosalind, she entirely conquered her love of idleness. She was really not deficient in natural capacity, and she soon began to take pleasure in trying to improve herself; so that when she returned to Maryland, she carried with her a newly acquired taste for rational pursuits, which she never afterwards lost.

MADELINE MALCOLM.

Well, Juliet, how is your friend, Cecilia Selden?" said Edward Lansdowne to his sister, as they were sitting by the parlour fire, in the interval between daylight and darkness. It was the evening after his arrival from Princeton college to spend a fortnight at Christmas with his family in Philadelphia.

Juliet. I believe Cecilia is very well. At least she was so when last I saw her, about five weeks since.

Edward. Is it five weeks since you have seen Cecilia Selden? You were formerly almost inseparable. I hope there has been no quarrel between you.

Juliet. None at all. But—somehow—I am tired of Cecilia Selden. She is certainly a very dull companion.

Edward. Dull! You once thought her very amusing. For my part, *I* always found her so. She has read a great deal, is highly accomplished, and as she travels every summer with her parents, she has had opportunities of seeing a variety of interesting places and people. And above all, she has an excellent natural understanding.

Juliet. But she is always so sensible and so correct, and every thing that she says and does is so very proper.

Edward. So much the better. You will improve by being intimate with her.

Juliet. I never shall be intimate again with Cecilia Selden. She is too particular, too fastidious. She does not like Madeline Malcolm.

Edward. And who is Madeline Malcolm? I never heard of her before.

Juliet. Her father is our next door neighbour. You know we did not live in this house when you were last in Philadelphia. The very day we moved, Madeline Malcolm came in to see us, in the midst of all our bustle and confusion, and stayed the whole afternoon. She said she had long been desirous of becoming acquainted with me, was delighted that we were now near neighbours, and therefore could not forbear running in to commence the intimacy immediately.

Edward. But "in the midst of all your bustle and confusion," it must have been very in convenient to receive a visitor, and to entertain her the whole afternoon.

Juliet. Why,—we were a little disconcerted at first, but she begged of us not to consider her a stranger. She was just as sociable as if she had known us for seven years; and she was so queer, and there was so much fun in every thing she said and did, that she kept me laughing all the time.

Edward. I should like to see this prodigy of fun.

Juliet. No doubt you will soon have that pleasure; for she runs in and out, the back way, ten times a-day.

Juliet had scarcely spoken when they heard a voice in the entry, singing "I'd be a butterfly," and Madeline Malcolm, a tall, black-eyed, red-cheeked girl, with long ringlets of dark hair, came flying into the parlour, exclaiming, "What, still by fire-light—I shall have to pull your Peter's ears myself, if he does not mind his business and light the astral lamp sooner. O! here he comes. Now, Peter, proceed; and take yourself off as soon as you have accomplished the feat. Well,—now that there is no longer any danger of falling over this young gentleman, I must beg leave to be introduced to him in form. I surmise that he is the most learned Mr. Edward Lansdowne of Nassau-Hall, Princeton. Ah! I have torn my frock on the fender. Just like me, you know." Juliet immediately introduced her brother. "Well, Ned," exclaimed Miss Malcolm, "you have come to make us happy at last. Your sister has talked so much about you that I have actually been longing for your arrival. Come, tell us the best news at college. I have a cousin there, but he has not been in town since the rebellion before the last. I suppose he goes to New York to take his frolics. Come, tell us all the particulars of your last 'Barring out;' I suppose it was conducted according to the newest fashion. Juliet, did you ever see any thing like Ned's face? A sort of mixed expression; trying to smile and be agreeable, but looking all the time as if he could bar *me* out himself."

In this manner she ran on for near half an hour, Juliet laughing heartily, and Edward not at all. At last she rose to go away, and when Juliet invited her to stay all the evening, she said she *must* go home, for they were to have waffles at tea, and she would not miss them on any consideration. However, the tea-table in Mrs. Lansdowne's parlour being now set, she took a spoonful of honey which she dripped all over the cloth, and then giving Juliet a hearty kiss, she seized Edward's arm saying, "Come, Ned, escort me home. I am going in at the front-door this time, and there is always ice on our steps, so be sure to take care that I do not fall."

When Edward took his leave at Madeline's door, she shook hands with him, saying, "Am I not a wild creature? You see how my spirits run away with me."

Edward came back with a countenance of almost disgust. "If this is your new friend," said he to his sister, "I must say that I consider her scarcely endurable. Why, she never saw me before this evening, and yet she is as familiar as if she had known me all her life. To think of her calling me Ned."

"Ah!" said Juliet with a smile, "I suspect *that* to be the grand offence, after all. But depend upon it, you will like her better when you know her better."

"I very much doubt my ever liking her at all," replied Edward.

Nothing could exceed the sociability of Madeline Malcolm. She breakfasted, dined, and drank tea at Mrs. Lansdowne's table nearly as often as at her father's; and she frequently ran in early in the morning, and scampered into Juliet's chamber before she had risen. Mr. and Mrs. Lansdowne (both whose dispositions were remarkably amiable and indulgent) did not approve of their daughter's intimacy with Madeline. They had spoken to her on the subject; but Madeline's frank and caressing manner, and her perpetual good-humour, had so won the heart of Juliet, that it was painful to her to hear a word against her friend, as she called her. So her parents concluded to let it pass for the present; trusting to Juliet's becoming eventually disgusted by some outrageous folly of Madeline's, who seemed to think her professed volatility an excuse for every thing; and that the appellation of *a wild creature*, which she took pride in giving herself, would screen her from any resentment her unwarrantable conduct might provoke.

Still, as Edward observed, she had a great deal of selfishness and cunning; as is generally the case with wild creatures; for when females have so little of the delicacy of their sex as to throw aside the restraints of propriety, the same want of delicacy makes them totally regardless of the feelings or convenience of others, and renders them callous to every thing like real sympathy or kindness of heart.

At home, Madeline was allowed to do exactly as she pleased; her father's thoughts were perpetually in his counting house, and her step-mother, who spent all her time in the nursery, was incessantly occupied with the care of a large family of young children, of whom Madeline never took the least account. And she was so much at Mr. Lansdowne's that Juliet had few opportunities of returning her visits.

She borrowed all Juliet's best books, and did not scruple to lend them again to any person that she knew. Some of the books were never returned; and others were brought back soiled, torn, and in a most deplorable condition. One of her jokes was to take up Juliet's muslin-work, and disfigure it with what she called gobble-stitch. She came in one day and found the parlour unoccupied, and Juliet's drawing-box on the table, with a beautiful landscape nearly finished. Madeline sat down and daubed at it till it was quite spoiled, and when Juliet discovered her at this employment, she turned it off with a laugh, insisting that she had greatly improved the picture. She found Juliet one evening engaged in copying a very scarce and beautiful song, which she had borrowed from her music-master, and which had never been published in America. On Juliet's being called up stairs for a few moments to her mother, Madeline took the pen, and scribbled on the margin of the borrowed music, some nonsensical verses of her own composition, in ridicule of the music-master.

Edward presented his sister at Christmas with a set of a new English magazine, which contained biographical sketches and finely engraved portraits of some of the most celebrated female authors. Madeline came in soon after the arrival of the books; and having looked them over, she insisted on carrying one of the volumes home with her. Next day she brought it back, with a pair of spectacles drawn with a pen and ink round the eyes of each of the portraits that, as she said, "The learned ladies might look still wiser." Upon this Edward immediately left the room, lest his indignation should induce him to say too much, and Juliet could not help warmly expressing her dissatisfaction. But Madeline pacified her by hanging round her neck and pleading that her love of fun was constantly leading her to do mischievous things; and that she was sure her darling Juliet loved her too well not to forgive her.

Cecilia Selden, a sensible and amiable girl, and formerly Juliet's most intimate friend, was an object of Madeline's particular dislike and ridicule; of which Cecilia perceived so many palpable symptoms, that she left off visiting at Mrs. Lansdowne's house; to the great regret of Edward.

Mrs. Templeton, a lady that lived at the distance of a few squares, gave a juvenile ball, to which Juliet and Edward were invited, and also Madeline with several of her little brothers and sisters. Soon after Juliet had gone up to her room to commence dressing, Madeline came in followed by a servant with two bandboxes, and exclaiming, "Well, Juliet, I have brought all my trappings, and have come here to dress with *you*, that I may escape being put in requisition at home to assist in decorating the brats, who will entirely fill up *our* carriage, so I am going to the ball in *yours*. There now, get away from the glass and let me begin."

Juliet removed from the glass, and throwing a shawl over her shoulders, sat down by the fire, determined to wait patiently till Madeline had finished her toilet. But this was no expeditious matter. Madeline always professed to be too giddy to have her clothes in order, or to think of any thing before the last moment. Every article that she was to wear this evening required some alteration, which Juliet was called upon to make, till Lucy, a mulatto seamstress that lived in the family, came up to assist the young ladies in dressing. Madeline's white satin under-frock was longer than the tulle dress that she wore over it: and after it was put on, it was necessary to make it shorter by turning the hem up all round and running it along with a needle and thread. Her satin belt would not meet, and after a great deal of pulling and squeezing in vain, the only remedy was to take off the hooks and eyes and set them nearer to the ends. She desired Lucy to arrange her hair for her, which was a difficult task, as Madeline would not hold still a moment; and after it was at last accomplished, she declared that Lucy had made a fright of her, and demolished the whole structure with her own hands, strewing the floor with hair-pins and flowers. She then called Juliet to her assistance; and, in the course of time, her hair was finished to her satisfaction.

When Madeline was dressed, she took a lamp from the mantlepiece and setting it on the floor, that she might see her feet to advantage with her embroidered silk stockings and white satin shoes, she began to caper and dance; and in performing one of her best steps she kicked down the lamp, which splashed all over her right foot, and over the lower part of her dress, beside deluging the carpet with oil. She screamed violently, and her volatility seemed to forsake her when she held up her beautiful tulle dress bespattered with lamp-oil. Juliet endeavoured to console her, and lent her another pair of silk stockings, and Lucy was sent to the nearest shoemaker's to bring several pair of white satin shoes that Madeline might choose from among them. But what was to be done with the disfigured frock? Madeline declared she had no other dress that was handsome enough to wear that evening, and said she would rather stay away from the ball than not look as she wished. Juliet, who was about the same size, offered to lend her a frock, even the clear muslin she was to wear that night herself; but Madeline said that Juliet's dresses were all too plain for her, and that she had set her mind upon the white silk-sprigged tulle, and nothing else.

She continued to lament her misfortune, when a thought struck her that it was possible to conceal the spots of oil by arranging artificial flowers round the lower part of the dress. But Juliet had no such flowers, not having yet begun to wear them, and her mother had long since left them off. Madeline's whole stock of flowers, was already disposed of on her head, and she protested against taking out a single one; saying, that it required a multitude to cover all the oil-stains.

At last she exclaimed, "I have just thought of it, Juliet,—There are plenty of flowers in the French vases on your front-parlour mantle-piece.ᴬ I will have *them*. They will do exactly."—"But," said Juliet, "I know not that my mother will approve of the flowers being taken out of the vases."—"Nonsense," replied Madeline. "What a vastly proper person you are. Tell her that your volatile friend Madeline took them; and she will expect nothing better of such a wild creature."

ᴬIt was formerly the fashion to decorate the mantle-piece with artificial flowers placed in china vases under glass shades.

So saying, she ran down stairs, and found Edward dressed for the ball, and waiting for them in the parlour. "Here, Ned, my boy," said she, "off with those glass shades, and hand me out the flowers from the vases. I have kicked over a lamp and splashed my frock with oil, and I must have all the flowers I can get, to hide the stains. Why do you look so dubious? I will send them safely back again to-morrow morning. What, won't you give them to me? Oh! then I shall make bold to help myself to them."—She jumped on a chair, and was going to lift one of the glass shades, when Edward, fearful of the consequences, stepped up and took out the flowers for her; and when she had obtained them all, she ran off with them in her lap, dropping them along the stairs as she went.

When she entered the chamber, she called out to Juliet, "Come now, dear creature, down on your knees with a pin-cushion in your hand, and pin these flowers all nicely round my frock, so as to cover every one of the vile oil-spots." "Shall *I* do it, miss?" said the maid, who had just finished wiping up the oil that had fallen on the carpet, and which, however, left a large splash of grease. "Miss Juliet will rumple her dress if she stoops down to put on the flowers."— "So much the better," said Madeline, "it will be an advantage to that new muslin to have a little of the stiffness taken out. Come, Lucy, you may hold the candle." Juliet then stooped down, and in a most painful posture proceeded to pin the flowers round Madeline's frock, which she did so adroitly as to conceal all the spots of oil.

Just as this business was completed a servant brought into the room a small red morocco case, inclosing a beautiful pearl necklace, and accompanied by a note from her grandfather, in which he requested her acceptance of it as a new-year's gift, and desired that she would wear it on that evening at Mrs. Templeton's ball.

While Juliet was admiring the necklace, Madeline took it out of her hand, saying, "Let me see how this looks on *my* neck. Beautiful—really beautiful. Ah, Juliet, it is so pretty I cannot bear to take it off again. Come *I* shall wear it this evening."—"But indeed," said Juliet, "I should like very much to wear it myself; particularly as it is my grandfather's request."—"Nonsense," answered Madeline; "grandpa is not going to the ball himself, and how will he know whether you wear it or not? And your father and mother are both at the theatre, and are ignorant even of its arrival. I forgot to bring a necklace with me: so this comes quite *apropos*. Come, I am not going to give it up this evening. Possession, you know, is nine points of the law: and your white neck requires no pearls to set it off."

"You know very well that my neck is *not* white," said Juliet.

"Well then," replied Madeline, "if it is brown, the pearls will make it look browner still. Positively you shall not have it to-night, if I run for it." Upon which she ran down stairs into the front-parlour, and pretended to hide behind the window-curtain, to save herself, as she told Edward, from the vengeance of Juliet, whose new necklace she had seized and carried off. Edward did not think this a very good joke; however, he made no comment, and his sister coming down immediately after, he handed her and Madeline into the carriage, and accompanied them to Mrs. Templeton's.

At the ball the volatility of Madeline reached its climax. She talked, laughed, flirted, jumped, and occasionally appealed to those in the same cotillon to know if they had ever seen such a wild creature. Edward, however, could not help observing her unkindness and rudeness to the little children, whom she pushed about and scolded, whenever they came in her way. Two of her younger sisters were preparing to dance together, when Madeline and Edward, who were looking for a place, came up. "This cotillon is completed," said Edward, "and so, I believe, are all the others. Let us stand by, and look on. I always enjoy seeing the children dance." "No indeed," said Madeline, "I had rather dance myself. Here, Ellen and Clara, go and sit down, and give us your places." The children began to object; but she pushed them away and commenced the cotillon, saying she was determined to dance every set.

The next set, however, no one asked Madeline to dance. She looked very much displeased at being obliged to sit still, and was yet more so, when Charles Templeton brought up a very handsome little midshipman, in his uniform, who, on being introduced to both the young ladies, immediately requested the pleasure of Miss Lansdowne's hand for the next set.

Juliet stood up with the midshipman; but there was some delay in forming the cotillons, and her partner perceived that one of his shoe-strings was broken. He asked Charles Templeton, who was in the next cotillon, if he would put him in a way of repairing the accident; and Charles desired the midshipman to accompany him to his room for the purpose. Madeline, who had heard all that passed, stepped up to Juliet and said to her—"Juliet, as you are one of the modest people, I suppose it will embarrass you to stand here till your partner comes back again; so do you sit down, and I will stand and keep your place for you. You know I have brass enough for any thing."

Juliet, grateful for Madeline's unexpected kindness, and feeling really some embarrassment at standing up in the cotillon without her partner, consented willingly, and took Madeline's seat. In a few minutes the midshipman returned, and looked much surprised when he saw another young lady in the place of his partner; but before he had time to consider why it was so, the music commenced, and Madeline began to right and left, and led off the cotillon; disappointing Juliet of her dance.

The midshipman, however, did not speak to Madeline during the whole set; and when he had led her to a seat, he left her, and went up to Edward, and expressed his surprise that Miss Lansdowne, after being engaged to dance with him, had substituted another young lady in her place. Edward, to whom his sister had explained how it happened, repeated her account to the midshipman, who was much vexed, and went immediately to apologize to Juliet, and to ask her hand for the next set, which she was obliged to refuse, as she was pre-engaged both for that set and the following.

"So," said Madeline, as she passed Juliet on her way to the cotillon with a new partner, "you see I tricked you out of the smart young midshipman, who is the prettiest fellow in the room, and I was determined not to sit still a single set."

Madeline's volatility attracted the attention of the whole company, and the delight of finding herself an object of general notice gave her fresh spirits as she ran to the very top of the country-dance, oversetting a little boy on her way, afterwards romping down the middle, and throwing herself into a seat the moment she had got to the bottom.

Soon after, while refreshments were handed round, she took an opportunity of purposely spilling a glass of lemonade on Cecilia Selden's pink crape frock, and she threw a piece of orange-peel in Edward's way that he might slip on it, which he did, and very nearly fell down.

Juliet, who had recently recovered from a severe cold, brought with her into the ball-room a very handsome blue silk scarf, which her mother had lent her, enjoining her to put it on whenever she was not dancing, as a guard against being suddenly chilled when in a perspiration. Madeline, happening to look at Juliet, observed the scarf and thought it very becoming. She suddenly twitched it off Juliet's shoulders and threw it over her own, saying, "Now, Juliet, you have been beautified with this scarf long enough. It is my turn to wear it awhile." Poor Juliet knew not how to object, though her seat (the only one she had been able to obtain) was directly against a window, from which there was a draught of air on the back of her neck. The consequence was a renewal of her cold, and a sore throat which confined her for several days to the house.

The above may serve as a specimen of Madeline's various exploits at the ball. After Juliet and her brother had got home, Edward stood for half an hour in the middle of the parlour-floor with his bed-candle in his hand, while he expostulated with his sister on her strange infatuation for her new friend; declaring that, with all her volatility and apparent frankness and good-humour, he had never known a girl more artful, selfish, and heartless than Madeline Malcolm.

Instead of returning the flowers and the necklace on the following morning, as she ought to have done, Madeline wore them in the evening to another ball; and finally when Mrs. Lansdowne sent for the flowers, they came home in a most deplorable state, soiled, crushed, and broken; so that they were no longer fit to ornament the vases, and some of them were entirely lost.

Madeline did not come in to see Juliet till she knew that she had quite recovered from her sore-throat; having, as she afterward told her, a perfect antipathy to a sick-room, and a mortal dislike to the dismals. She forgot to return the necklace till Juliet, with many blushes, and much confusion, at last reminded her of it. "Why," said she, "you seem very uneasy about that necklace. Between friends like us, every thing ought to be common." Madeline, however, had never offered to lend Juliet the smallest article belonging to herself.

The next time Madeline came, she brought the necklace in her hand. "Here," said she "is this most important affair; I took a fancy to wear it round my *head* at Mrs. Linton's, and I can assure you I had a great deal of pulling and stretching to get it to clasp. Why did grandpapa give you such a short necklace? However, soon after I began to dance, snap went the thread, and down came all the pearls showering about the floor. How I laughed; but I set all the beaux in the cotillon to picking them up, and I suppose they found the most of them. You see I have brought you a handful. And now you can amuse yourself with stringing them again. Come now, don't look so like Ned.—How can you expect a wild creature as I am, to be careful of flowers, and beads, and all such trumpery? I dare say, you are now thinking that your sober Cecilia Selden would have returned the pearls 'in good order and well conditioned.' But I never allow any one to get angry with me: you know I am a privileged person. So now look agreeable, and smile immediately. Smile, smile, I tell you." Juliet *did* smile, and Madeline throwing her arms round her neck, kissed her, exclaiming, as she patted her cheek, "There's my own good baby. She always, at last, does as I bid her."

The next day Juliet heard that the windows of Mr. Malcolm's house were all shut up; but she was not long in suspense as to the cause, for shortly after, Madeline came running in the back way, and said with a most afflicted countenance, "O, Juliet, you may pity me now if you never did before. We have just heard from New Orleans of the death of aunt Medford, my father's only sister."

Juliet. I am very sorry you have received such bad news.

Madeline. Oh! but the worst of it is, that it will prevent our going to the play to-night. We had engaged seats with the Rosemores, in a delightful box. We were going to see the Belle's Stratagem, with the masquerade, and the song, and the minuet, and the new French dancers. I would not have missed such an entertainment for a hundred dollars. How very provoking that the bad news did not arrive one day later. If it had not come till to-morrow I should not have cared, for then our charming evening at the theatre would have been over. And now, to think that instead of going to the play, I must stay at home and look at my father grieving for old aunt Medford. There now, Juliet, your face is again in the style of Ned's. Positively, if you are so particular, I shall cut your acquaintance. Those that I consider my friends must enter into all my "whims and oddities," and not expect me to act according to rule. I hate hypocrisy. Why should I pretend to grieve for aunt Medford when I have never seen her since I was six years old?

Juliet. But sympathy for your father—

Madeline. Why, where is the use of sympathy? When people are in grief, sympathy only makes them worse.

Juliet. If you yourself were in affliction, Madeline, you would find the sympathy of your family and friends very gratifying.

Madeline. Wait till *I am* in affliction and then I will tell you. "*Toujours gai,*" is my motto, and "*vive la bagatelle*" for ever.

So saying, she danced out of the room, and went home; but in a short time she returned, looking very mysterious, and peeping in at the door to ascertain if Juliet was alone. "Juliet, love," said Madeline in a low voice, "come with me into the back parlour, lest we should be interrupted. I have something of great consequence to tell you."

As Madeline often dealt in mysteries, Juliet thought this new secret nothing more than usual, and accompanied her into the back parlour, where Madeline cautiously bolted the folding-doors and locked the side door. "Now, Juliet," said she in an under voice, "I know I may depend on your secrecy." "Certainly you may," replied Juliet.

Madeline. Well then, I must confide to you a plan that has just struck me. I cannot bear the idea of giving up the play to-night, and you know it is out of the question for any of the family to be *seen* there.

Juliet. Of course none of you can go to the theatre when your house is shut up for the death of a near relation, and when Mr. Malcolm is in such deep affliction.

Madeline. It is certainly a great pity that aunt Medford died; particularly just at the time she did, as it will spoil all our gayety for the winter. No more plays, and balls, and parties this season. People ought always to die in the summer. But you know, dear Juliet, I have not seen my aunt Medford for ten years, and I really have forgotten all about her. So, how can you expect me to be inconsolable? And I cannot endure the thought of being disappointed in going to the theatre. I might as well go, as stay at home and think about it all the evening.

Juliet. O no, indeed! Even if you have no personal regard for your aunt, respect for your father's feelings and a proper regard for decorum, ought to subdue your desire of going at this time to a place of public amusement.

Madeline. That is exactly such a speech as Cecilia Selden would make on a similar occasion. It is a pity "the truly wise man" is not here. How Neddy would applaud.

Juliet. But where is the use of talking in this manner. You know you *cannot* go to the theatre.

Madeline. I know I *can.*

Juliet. How? In what way? I do not understand you.

Madeline. My going to the theatre to-night depends principally on *you.*

Juliet. On me!

Madeline. Yes, for I will not venture alone, and you must go with me.

Juliet. Go with you—*I* go with you!

Madeline. Yes.

Juliet. And who else?

Madeline. Nobody else. Now don't look as if you were ready to run through the wall to get away from me; but listen and understand. Our nursery-maid, Kitty, has permission to go this evening and stay all night with a sick sister. So when she is off, I can easily slip into her room and select a suit of her clothes, (which I believe will nearly fit me,) and she has a tolerably large wardrobe for a servant. Then I will steal in the back way, bringing a suit for you. Don't look shocked. I shall tell my father and mother that being very low-spirited, I am coming in here to spend a quiet evening with you. I heard Mrs. Lansdowne, when I was here yesterday, propose to your father to leave her at her sister, Mrs. Wilmar's, on his way to the Wistar party to-night, and call for her as he comes back; which of course will not be before ten o'clock at the very earliest. Therefore the coast will be clear, as I suppose Ned will go to his beloved Athenæum. So you see every thing seems to conspire fortunately to forward our plot.

Juliet. Our plot. O! do not call it *ours.* I never will have any thing to do with a plot.

Madeline. Yes, but you *must* though. Why this is nothing. I have plotted a hundred things in the course of my life, and so I shall again. Well, now hear the whole. I will slip in the back-way, and you must be alone in your room ready to receive me. After we have put on our disguises, we will go down stairs very softly and steal out at the alley gate. Then we will make the best of our way to the theatre, and go in at the gallery-door, passing, of course as two servant-girls. When we have reached the gallery we will mix with the crowd, and sit at our ease and enjoy the play; at least the masquerade-scene, which I would not miss for the world. I am absolutely dying to see the French dancers. Nobody can possibly discover us under our disguises. We will not go till the first act is over, and the audience settled; and we will come away before the last scene of the comedy. Then after we get home we will resume our proper dresses, and present ourselves to our parents, looking as demure as if we had been sitting by the fire, and talking sensibly, all the evening. No one will ever know what we have really been doing. It will be a most charming frolic, and something for you and I to laugh about, ten years hence. I always enjoy these queer exploits that no one else has courage to undertake.

Juliet (*firmly.*) Madeline, I will *not* disguise myself like a servant-girl; and I will *never* accompany you secretly to the theatre, nor to any other place.

Juliet spoke in so firm a tone, that Madeline was at first abashed, and remained for a few moments silent. But, not easily repelled, she soon recovered from her confusion, and exerted all her eloquence to prevail on her dear friend, as she called her, to join in the scheme. By turns she flattered, caressed, and ridiculed her, and then tried to win her consent by representing the delights of the masquerade-scene, as she had heard it described by a lady who had recently seen the comedy of the Belle's Stratagem. Juliet held out steadily for a long time. But at length her firmness gave way, and she finally yielded; as Madeline had foreseen. Her reluctance was so great, that her consent was, after all, rather extorted than given, and Madeline, having kissed her rather oftener than usual, ran gayly to her own home, singing "I won't be a nun."

After Madeline had gone, Juliet felt so uneasy at having suffered herself to be persuaded against her conscience, that she was on the point of calling her back and retracting her promise. When she went to dinner, the consciousness of her intended deceit destroyed her appetite, and made her feel as if she could not raise her eyes towards her parents, or answer them when they spoke to her.

Edward bent on her a scrutinizing glance, and saw that all was not right; but supposing that she had committed some fault in the course of the morning for which her mother had seriously reprimanded her, he was unwilling to notice her apparent mortification, and tried to divert the attention of his parents by talking to them of Cooper's last novel, which had been published that morning, and of which he had already gone through the first volume.

Mrs. Lansdowne, however, remarking that her daughter did not eat, inquired if she felt unwell, and Juliet replied that she had a violent headache: which was literally true. After dinner, her mother recommended that she should retire to her room and lie down, which she gladly did: her mind being too much agitated to take interest in any occupation. Once in the afternoon, she heard Edward come up stairs and tap at her door; but fearing that he had observed her confusion at dinner, and that he might ask her some question concerning it, she lay still, and did not answer to his knock, so that, supposing her to be asleep, he softly withdrew.

Towards evening, her mother came to inquire after her: and Juliet, unwilling to meet the family at table in her present state of discomposure, requested to have her tea sent up. "My dear," said Mrs. Lansdowne, "as you are not well, I will not go to my sister Wilmar's this evening, but I will stay at home and sit with you."

"O, no, dear mother!" replied Juliet, "I know you wish to see aunt Wilmar: I am sure my tea will relieve my headache, and I have no doubt, when I have drunk it, I shall feel well enough to rise, and sit up all the evening." Accordingly, after Juliet had taken her tea, she rose and adjusted her dress, and when Mrs. Lansdowne came up again, she found her daughter sitting by the fire with a book, and apparently so much recovered, that she felt no scruples about leaving her, as she was really desirous of passing the evening with Mrs. Wilmar, who was confined to the house with the influenza.

At last Juliet heard her father and mother depart, and Edward went out soon after. In a few minutes, Madeline came cautiously up stairs, and glided into the chamber, carrying a large bundle. "All's safe," said she, "the coast is *quite* clear, and we have not a moment to lose. It is a fine moonlight night."

Juliet's courage now failed entirely; and she vehemently besought Madeline to give up a scheme fraught with so much risk and impropriety. But Madeline was immovable, declaring that she had set her heart on it, and that she enjoyed nothing so much as what she called an out-of-the-way frolic. "Since you are so cowardly, Juliet," said she, "I wish I could venture to go alone; but wild as I am, I confess I am not quite equal to that—Come, now, off with your frock, and get yourself dressed in these delectable habiliments."

She then began to unfasten Juliet's dress, who pale, trembling, and with tears in her eyes, arrayed herself in the clothes that Madeline had brought for her. The gown was a very dirty one of dark blue domestic gingham, and she put on with it a yellowish chequered handkerchief, and a check apron. Over this she pinned an old red woollen shawl, and she covered her head with a coarse and broken black Leghorn bonnet. The clothes that Madeline had allotted to herself were a little better, consisting of a dark calico frock, a coarse tamboured muslin collar, an old straw bonnet very yellow and faded, and a plaid cloak which belonged to the cook, and which she had taken out of a closet in the garret.

The two young ladies did not know, or did not recollect, that when *real* servant-girls go to the theatre, they generally dress as well as they can, and take pains to appear to the best advantage. The clothes that Madeline had selected were quite too dirty and shabby for the occasion. To complete their costume, she gave Juliet a pair of coarse calf-skin shoes, which were so large that as she walked her feet seemed to rise up out of them. Madeline, for her part, put on a pair of carpet-moccasins over her slippers.

After they were dressed and ready to depart for the theatre, Juliet's tremor increased, and she was again on the point of relinquishing her share in the business; but she again yielded to the solicitations of Madeline, who led her softly down stairs by the light of the moon that shone in at the staircase windows. They stole, undiscovered, across the yard and out at the alley-gate; and finding themselves in the street, began to walk very fast, as people generally do when they are going to the play.

When they came in view of the theatre, they saw no persons there, except two or three gentlemen who went in at the pit-door. Juliet's heart failed entirely; and she shrank back as Madeline, taking her hand, attempted to pull her towards the door that admitted the gallery-people. "We have now gone too far to recede," whispered Madeline,—"You must stand by me now. I *will not* go back, and *you must* come forward. Here, take my money and put it down with yours—I forgot my gloves, and my hands will betray me, so I must keep them wrapped up in my cloak."

Juliet laid the money on the ledge before the doorkeeper, who looked at them with some surprise. They pulled their bonnets more closely over their faces, and passed up the stairs; Madeline running as fast as possible, and Juliet entreating her in a low voice to stop a little, as she could not keep pace with her. They soon found themselves in the gallery, and being assisted over the benches by a very polite black man, they took their seats among some coloured people about the centre of the middle row.

The crowd and heat were intolerable. Juliet kept her eyes cast down; afraid to look round the house, or even to steal a glance towards the stage. Madeline, however, looked round boldly, and in a few minutes, to her great consternation, she perceived Edward Lansdowne standing up in the back part of one of the stage-boxes. Having finished his novel, and feeling no inclination to read any more that night, he had concluded to go to the theatre, reminded of it by seeing the bill in the evening paper. "Juliet," whispered Madeline, "there is my evil genius." "Where, where?" exclaimed Juliet, thrown almost off her guard. "If we can distinguish *him* at so great a distance, he can also discover *us*."—"You forget," replied Madeline, "that we are in disguise." These words, though uttered in a whisper, were evidently heard by the people round, who all turned to look at them; and some tried to peep under their bonnets, which made Juliet draw hers down over her face till her sight was entirely obscured by it.

The play went on; but Madeline and Juliet could not enjoy it, all their attention being engaged by the continual fear of discovery. Juliet, however heard enough to convince her that her parents would never have taken her to see the Belle's Stratagem; as when they did indulge her with a visit to the theatre, they always selected a night when the play was unexceptionable, and the whole entertainment such as a young lady could witness with propriety.

At length came the masquerade-scene, and in a short time the French dancers appeared. Just then, a short, fat, red-faced and very vulgar Englishwoman who sat behind Madeline and Juliet, gave each of them a twitch on the shoulder, saying, in a broad Yorkshire dialect, "I'll thank you gals or ladies or whatsomdever you be, to take off your bunnets and let a body have some chance of seeing the show; for I've been popping my ead back and furrads atween you ever sence you comed hin, and thof I've as good a right to see as any body else, I've ardly got a squint at the hactors yet."

The girls were now in a most critical dilemma. To take off their bonnets seemed out of the question, as the exposure of their heads would no doubt betray them, and their fear and perplexity were so great that they had not presence of mind either to speak or move.

"Don't pertend that you don't ear me," said the Englishwoman, giving them both a hard push forward with her huge hands. "I bees a true King Georgeswoman, and won't be put upon by none of the Yankees, not I, thof I *am* come to their country. I pays my money as well as you, and I've jist as good a right to see the show; and if you won't take off them big bunnets, I'll be bound I'll make you, if there's even a row about it. I've raised a row afore this time when I've been put upon."

"Oh! let us go, let us go," said Juliet, gasping with terror, and seizing Madeline's arm.

"Honly wait," continued the Englishwoman, "till I tells my usband, who sets ahind here, to call 'turn 'em out.' You *may* be ladies. But I bees an onest oman, and if I've come to a land of liberty, the more reason that I should make free to speak my mind; and if we're all hequal, why then nobody han't no right to put upon me."

By this time the two girls, in an agony of trepidation, had scrambled over the benches and got to the door, expecting every instant to hear the dreaded words, "turn them out," and to see Edward's eyes directed towards them, with those of the whole audience. Scarcely conscious of what they were doing, they ran down the gallery-stairs, and flew out of the door into the street. As is usual toward the latter part of the play, a number of boys had collected about the fruit-stalls waiting for checks, that they might gain admittance to see the farce; and as Madeline ran past them, her cloak flew open, and the moonbeams shone brightly on a brilliant ring which she always wore on her fore-finger. This with something in their appearance that would cause even unpractised eyes to suspect that they were young ladies, attracted the attention of the boys, who stared at them with surprise and curiosity.

Madeline and Juliet ran down the street in breathless terror. They had gone about a square from the theatre before they recollected that their way home lay in a contrary direction, and that they ought to go *up* the street instead of *down.* "Oh! we are going *from* home instead of *towards* it," exclaimed Juliet; and they immediately turned about and ran up Chestnut street. They again passed the theatre, terrified, bewildered, their bonnets falling back and discovering their frightened faces in full view; Madeline's cloak half untied and flying out behind her, and Juliet still grasping one corner of her shawl (which had fallen entirely off her shoulders) and dragging it after her along the pavement. On seeing them running back in this forlorn condition, the boys set up a loud shout, and calling out "Hurrah for the ladies," pursued them up Chestnut street.

A young gentleman who had left the theatre a few minutes before, and was walking leisurely up the street, turned round to discover the meaning of all the noise that was coming after him, and caught Juliet, breathless and almost dead, by her two hands. "Juliet," he exclaimed, "my sister Juliet!" "Oh, Edward!" she shrieked, and fell into his arms drowned in tears.

"Save me, save me," cried Madeline, catching him by the coat. "Madeline too!" said Edward. "What does all this mean?"

Another gentleman now came up, and ordered off the boys, reprimanding them severely for chasing two unprotected females; and Edward taking one of the girls under each arm, walked on in silence, much affected by the sobbing of Juliet.

Madeline soon recovered herself, and attempted an explanation of the strange predicament in which he had found them; passing it off as a very good joke, and a further proof of her ungovernable volatility.

Edward remained silent. He would not reproach her, but he determined in his mind what course to pursue. He took leave of Madeline at her own door, and on entering his father's house, he told Juliet that she had better, as soon as possible, divest herself of her disguise. Juliet could not speak, but she wept on her brother's shoulder; and Edward kissed her cheek, and bade her good night.

She retired to bed, but she could not sleep; and in the morning she rose earlier than usual, and went into the parlour, where she knew she would find Edward. She looked very pale, and her eyes were swimming in tears. "Oh! Edward," said she, "what did my father and mother say, when they came home last night, and you told them all that happened?"

"I told them nothing," replied Edward, "I love you too well to betray you. I have kept your secret, and I shall never disclose it. But I must have a recompense."

Juliet. Any, any recompense, dearest Edward. What can you ask that I could possibly refuse.

Edward. I require you, from this day, to give up all acquaintance with Madeline Malcolm. Your infatuation for a girl who, under the name of wildness and volatility, sets all propriety at defiance, is to me astonishing. Henceforward let there be no more intimacy between you. It must be checked before it leads to consequences still worse than the adventures of last night.

Juliet. I acknowledge that Madeline is too regardless of decorum, and that she says and does many strange and improper things: but then she has so good a heart.

Edward. Tell me one proof of it. You have fallen into the common error of supposing that all persons who profess to be giddy, wild, and reckless, have kind feelings and good hearts. On the contrary, they may too often be classed with the most selfish, cold, and heartless people in the world; for they have seldom either sense or sensibility, and while resolutely bent on the gratification of their own whims, are generally regardless of the peace and convenience of those about them. When I first went to college I thought as you do. I supposed that the most careless, noisy, and desperate boys must necessarily have kind and generous feelings. But I found the contrary to my cost; and I am now convinced, that, with some few exceptions, the best hearts are generally united with the best heads and the best manners.

Juliet. But even if I never visit Madeline myself, how shall I prevent her running in to me as she does, two or three times a day?

Edward. Very easily. Write her a concise note, intimating that you do not consider it proper to continue your acquaintance with her.

Juliet. Oh! Edward, I never can do that.

Edward. Is not this the recompense I am entitled to, for keeping your secret?

Juliet. Indeed, Edward, you are too cruel.

Edward. Severe, perhaps, but not cruel. The exigency of the case requires decisive measures. "I am cruel only to be kind," and you will thank me for it hereafter.

Juliet. Well then, I *will* write the note. And if it *must be done* I will do it immediately; for if I allow myself to think about it long, it will grieve me so much that I shall never have resolution to go through with it. (*She goes to the desk and writes.*) There now, Edward, read this note.

Edward, (*reading.*) "Though convinced that it is better our intimacy should cease, it is not without regret that I decline all further intercourse with Madeline Malcolm. For her health and happiness I offer my best wishes; but in future we can only meet as strangers.

"Juliet Lansdowne."

Now seal and send it.

Juliet. Oh, Edward! it is hard to give up Madeline. But I believe you are right, and I ought not to regret it.

Edward. I *know* I am right.

Juliet then rang the bell for a servant, to whom with a quivering lip and hesitating hand she gave the note, desiring him to leave it next door for Miss Malcolm.

After breakfast, when Juliet was again alone with her brother, she said to him, "Edward, I have never yet concealed any thing from my parents. I think if I were to disclose to them the whole truth, I should feel less miserable."

Edward approved of this determination, and they went together to their mother, to whom Juliet candidly related the whole history of their going to the theatre in disguise. She kindly endeavoured to throw as little blame on Madeline as possible; and Edward tried to apologize for Juliet's partiality for this dangerous girl, and for the yielding gentleness of disposition with which his sister had allowed herself to be influenced by her; and for her want of judgment in not perceiving the faults of Madeline in as strong a light as they appeared to every one else.

Mrs. Lansdowne's pleasure, on finding that her daughter had consented to give up this very improper intimacy, counterbalanced her regret at Juliet's having been persuaded by Madeline to join in the folly and indecorum of the preceding evening. For this, however, she thought the girls had been sufficiently punished by all they had suffered at the theatre, and during their ignominious flight from it.

In the spring, Mr. Malcolm removed with his family to New York, and their house next door to Mr. Lansdowne's was immediately taken by the father of Cecilia Selden who had again become the intimate friend of Juliet.

THE END.